BAD PRINCE

ROYALLY UNEXPECTED: BOOK 1

LILIAN MONROE

WANT THREE BOOKS DELIVERED STRAIGHT TO YOUR INBOX?
HOW ABOUT THREE ROCK STAR ROMANCES THAT WERE *WAY* TOO
HOT TO SELL?

GET THE COMPLETE *ROCK HARD* SERIES:
WWW.LILIANMONROE.COM/ROCKHARD

1

ELLE

THE RHYTHMIC SQUEAKING of my housemate's bedsprings gets louder as the sound of her first moan floats through the wall. I stuff my earplugs in deeper, hoping they'll help block out the noise—even though I already know they won't. Dahlia's headboard taps against our shared wall. It starts gently, barely grazing the thin separation between our bedrooms.

And then it gets louder, and louder, and louder...

... until the wall actually *shakes*.

Another moan sounds out and a man says something barely audible. I assume it's something filthy. Dahlia, my best and weirdest friend, likes it dirty.

Why do I know this?

Because I hear everything in this rundown, mouse-infested house of ours.

Everything.

Groaning, I turn to my side, stuffing my pillow over my head to try to muffle the noise. I check the time on my phone. It's already past midnight, and I have to be up in four hours for crew practice. I'm going to be out on the water, rowing my little heart out as I train for the biggest regatta of my life, with less than four hours' sleep.

Sunday is—or rather, *was*— my day off, as usual, and Monday practices are notoriously tough after a rest day. Coach Bernard doesn't tolerate lateness, sleepiness, or excuses like *my roommate is a sex maniac.*

The banging on the wall continues, and my blood pressure rises. Every knock on the wall cranks my nerves tighter.

Bang. Bang. Bang.

Moan.

Bang. Bang. Bang.

Moan.

Dahlia goes to Farcliff University, too, but she's far from athletic—well, not in the traditional sense of the word. She runs her own athletics department from the comfort of her own bed.

No, Dahlia doesn't need to wake up at four o'clock in the morning, or practice twice a day, six days a week. She doesn't need to manage her protein intake down to the gram, or make sure her performance is stellar every single day just to keep her scholarship.

Unlike me, Dahlia can have manic, crazy sex every night of the week until the sun comes up...

... and she does.

When her voice goes up a couple octaves and a scream finally pierces the partition, I've had enough. My frustration boils over and I clamber onto my knees on the bed, banging my fist against the paper-thin wall so hard my knuckles bruise.

"Come on, you idiot! Make her come already!"

The squeaking stops. The moans pause.

Silence.

Then, the bead creaks once more as their weight shifts,

and peals of laughter sound through the wall. I slump back down on my own bed, exhaling as I rub my hands over my face.

If Dahlia wasn't the friendliest person I'd ever met—and if I could afford to live somewhere other than this rodent-plagued sex den—I'd definitely move out.

Unfortunately, though, I'm stuck here.

They move to the floor, thankfully. The floorboards aren't nearly as noisy as the bed.

BLEARY-EYED AND GRUMPY, I somehow make it to practice on time. In the locker room, I pull on my thermal, skin-hugging workout tights. My sports bra has so many straps and support mechanisms that it looks like it was designed by NASA for a trip to outer space.

I strap the bra on and adjust it, locking the girls down nice and securely. When I pull on my workout top and lean over to shove my bag in my locker, I feel the chill of the air over my lower back. Clothes never fit properly over my tall, athletic body, but I'm used to it by now.

I used to hate my height when I was a kid. As a teenager, I'd see all the boys going gaga over petite, delicate little waifs —and I felt like an ogre in comparison. Then I grew these massive knockers and I hated them, too, because all the boys went gaga over my boobs and forgot that there was a person attached to them.

I've always been taller, broader, and stronger than most men. My size isn't great for my love life, if I'm honest—I get friend zoned more often than I'd like to admit.

But my height means I can row. When I'm rowing, my breasts can be strapped down and kept out of the way. My rowing scholarship allows me to attend Farcliff University, where I'll hopefully make something of myself—and I wouldn't trade that opportunity for anything. With just over a year left until I graduate, I can honestly say that rowing has been my ticket out of a shitty, dead-end Grimdale life.

Would I like a gaggle of boyfriends to follow me around like a parade of little ducklings? Sure—why not? But am I going to stop rowing to get them?

Hell no.

Someone opens the locker room door and a blast of cold air whips through the room. I shiver, but I know as soon as I get out onto the water and start rowing, I'll be warm.

Then, a nasally, pretentious voice pierces my ears. My lips turn downward.

"Did you get your invitation yet?" Olivia Brundle's falsetto voice makes my stomach turn. I was hoping I wouldn't have to deal with her this early in the morning—at least not until after I'd been on the water.

"Got it last night," Olivia's clone, Marielle Davenport, replies. "What are you going to wear?"

"Well, Charlie likes it when I wear something that shows off my legs," Olivia says. She comes into view around the corner, flicking her long blonde hair over her shoulder. "So I'll probably wear something short, or at least something with a thigh-high slit." She titters, checking her nails.

Charlie.

Even at four o'clock in the goddamn morning, Olivia is name-dropping the Crown Prince of Farcliff. She talks about him as if they're engaged already, even though Dahlia told me Olivia has only met him once before at a state event four years ago. Olivia's father is the Prime Minister of Brundle, our neighbors to the south, so not only is she supremely annoying, but she's also been told that she's important since the day she was born.

4

Wonderful.

I tie my shoelaces loosely, knowing I'll take them off as soon as my boat is in the water. I stand up, and Olivia steps into my path.

"Did you get your invitation to the Prince's Ball, Elle?" She arches her perfectly groomed eyebrow and taps the side of her face with a manicured finger.

I don't answer.

"Is that a no?" Olivia glances at Marielle, grinning, before turning back to me. "Oh, right, you're just here as a charity case." She laughs, and Marielle follows suit.

I try to step around Olivia, but she moves with me. Her expensive perfume wafts toward me as she blocks my path. She's infuriating—right down to her long hair, curled into perfect, beachy waves that fall all the way down to her waist.

Seriously, who has time to curl their hair this early in the morning? I can just about manage to run a comb through my hair, and it's so short it barely gets tangled to begin with.

As I take another step to the side, Olivia mirrors my movements again to stop me.

"What, cat got your tongue?"

"I just want to practice, Olivia. You already know I haven't gotten an invite to that stupid party."

Marielle snorts. *Her* beachy blonde waves are already tied back in a high ponytail. The look she gives me is just as withering as Olivia's. "Stupid party? Elle, this isn't a 'stupid party'. This is where Prince Charlie chooses a wife."

I bite back my laughter, looking between the two of them. Everyone talks about the Prince's twenty-fifth birthday ball as if it's some magical, mystical, marriage-inducing event.

It's a freaking party—and a pretentious one at that.

Marielle and Olivia blink, staring at me.

"Wait, what? Are you being serious?" I scoff. "He chooses

a wife at this ball? Is this the Middle Ages? It's his birthday party."

They roll their eyes in unison, like two creepy plastic dolls.

"Fucking peasants," Olivia says, finally brushing past me. She takes care not to let any part of her body touch any part of mine, as if I'm some diseased leper.

"Pathetic. Of course she wouldn't understand, Ollie, she's from Grimdale." Marielle turns her big blue eyes to me. "Things are done differently in Farcliff, Elle. We actually have this thing called *class*. You should look it up."

She saunters past me without another look.

Rage.

My blood boils. My face turns beet red. Every stupid day of every stupid week, I'm made to feel like *less*. Less womanly. Less intelligent. Less worthy. Just... *less*.

Grimdale is only half an hour's drive away, but I might as well be from another planet for the way I'm treated here. It's not just Olivia and Marielle, either. All my teammates never waste an opportunity to make me feel like I don't belong here —like working my ass off for this stupid scholarship was a waste of time, because I'll never be accepted into this world no matter how hard I try.

I stomp out of the locker room and down to the warm-up area, even though my body is already burning hot. Olivia and Marielle will take their time to change their clothes and re-apply their makeup.

Yes, they need to *re*-apply their makeup before dawn. I'll never understand it.

I'm not complaining, though. It'll give me time to warm up and make my way to the shells on my own.

I heave a single scull onto my shoulder and grab my oars. The weight of the boat is already starting to calm me down.

Thank goodness I row singles, because I might not be able to resist capsizing us if I had to share a boat with either of those two egotistical, uppity little turds.

Coach Bernard is already waiting at the pier. He watches me put the shell in the water and set the oars in place. I keep my head down, not wanting to look up at the massive, stone building across the lake. Farcliff Castle looms above me, visible from almost everywhere on the university grounds. It's just one more stark reminder of how much I don't belong here. I'll always be the orphan girl from Grimdale, even if I do get this expensive, overrated university degree.

Coach clears his throat. "Everything okay?"

"Everything's fucking peachy, Coach." I kick my shoes off and set them on the shore before walking back toward my shell. My boat shoes are waiting for me at the end of the timber pier.

Coach looks at me under his dark, wiry eyebrows. He's assessing me—mentally, physically, emotionally—just like he does with all his athletes. I take a deep breath and square my shoulders, meeting his steely gaze. He drills his eyes into mine for a moment, then nods and looks down at his clipboard, satisfied.

"We're going for a steady, long interval practice today, Elle." Coach checks his notes.

I sweep my hand through my short brown hair, pushing it off my forehead. Between last night's sex party in Dahlia's room and this morning's encounter with the evil blonde twins, I'm having trouble focusing.

"Nice and easy," he continues. "I want you doing nine-minute 2k intervals. We're doing ten of them, so I hope you're nice and rested. It's going to be a long practice today. Here." He hands me the small headset I wear to hear his commands.

I slip my boat shoes on and get into the shell. The boat

rocks from side to side and I take a deep breath to calm myself down. The last thing I need is a dip in the lake at this hour.

When I'm set up near the marker buoys, I look up at Coach Bernard. His voice comes through the headset. *"All ready..."*

I grip the oars and close my eyes for the briefest moment. Inhaling deeply, I take in the scent of the water and the smell of the trees that line the shore. I savor the fresh, crisp taste of the air as it fills my lungs. My shell feels steady beneath me. My muscles coil in anticipation as I wait for my coach's command.

"Row."

My oars bite the water.

This is where I'm meant to be. I may be from Grimdale, and I may never get fancy little invitations to fancy little parties. I know I'll never become 'Charlie's' wife—or even see the Prince face-to-face—but I can row.

As my shell shears through the water, my whole body moves in sync—from my breath, through every muscle, and right down to the boat that supports me.

My height doesn't bother me here. On the water, it's an advantage. With every breath, I pull the oars through the water and sweep them back again, the blades almost skimming the glassy surface of Farcliff Lake. My body folds and extends with each stroke, and I'm free.

If I could fly, I imagine it would feel like this. It's effortless, smooth.

It's magic.

The air rushes around my body as my blood starts to pump. After two minutes, I'm nice and warm and I find my rhythm.

And I soar.

"*Wave left,*" Coach says in my ear as a power boat passes by, leaving a wake for me to deal with. It doesn't bother me— I'm in my element. This is what I was made to do.

I was born to row.

By the eight-minute mark, my breath is ragged and my legs and arms are screaming with that sweet, sharp burn that I've grown addicted to. I must be close to the 2000-meter mark by now.

"*Three hundred.*"

I pull, and I forget about the lack of sleep and the harpies in the locker room. I forget about Dahlia and the fact that her healthy sex life is the exact opposite of my own nun-like existence. I even forget that I wish it wasn't.

I just do what I do best. I row.

2

CHARLIE

THE SHARP CRACK of skin on skin has to be one of my favorite sounds in the universe. I leave a big red handprint on the chick's ass and she moans into my silk pillowcase.

"Yes, Prince! Yes," the girl screams as I rut her, rewarding her with another smack of my palm. She'll feel that one for days, and she'll probably show all her friends where Prince Charlie's hand left a mark on her perky little backside.

She twists backward to look at me, raising her hand and pressing it against my chest. Her lily-white arm is like a blank canvas against my tattooed chest. I yank her hand off my skin and curl it behind her back, holding it there and grunting as I thrust inside her even harder. When I empty my balls inside the girl with a loud moan, I only take a second to let the shivers of pleasure course through me.

Then, I pull the condom off my still-hard cock and tie it off securely. I roll off the girl and pad to my ensuite bathroom. There, I key in a code to my locked trashcan and drop the condom in with the three others we've already used since last night.

Hey—call me paranoid, but a prince has to do what a

prince has to do. I'm not going to get caught out with little Prince Charlies running around all over the place. My father was very clear about that—no illegitimate children.

Fine by me. I've almost been burned before, and I'm not going to let it happen again.

I walk back into my bedroom, naked as the day I was born. The girl—what was her name again?—rolls over and gives me a little whimper. She runs her fingers up her side and cups her own breast, giggling.

"That was nice, Your Highness."

I lean over to pick up the dress she wore to the club last night. I toss it to her.

"I have to get up, and you have to leave."

"But—"

"Nev will show you out." The door opens and my butler, Neville, appears. He gives me a deep bow and turns to face the girl. She's scrambling to cover herself with the sheet, and I flick my eyes at Nev, issuing an unspoken command.

He turns his back to her, giving the girl some semblance of privacy. As she scrambles to get dressed, I head back to the bathroom to wash the smell of sex off my body.

After a quick rinse, I pull on my running clothes and head for the door. The girl is gone, thank fuck. Nev got rid of her in record time. I need to give that man a raise.

If I'm lucky, I won't have to speak to anyone else for a few hours. I wind my way through the corridors of the castle, walking faster as I hear footsteps approaching. Only a few more seconds, and I'll be able to duck into a side passage that leads straight outside and onto the trails...

... but I'm not so lucky.

Talin, my father's right-hand man, steps around the corner and across my path.

"Your Highness," he says, giving me the smallest of bows

—barely inclining his head. His dark hair is slicked back and his eyes are razor-sharp. He gestures down the hallway. "Your father would like to have a word."

"Are you his little lapdog now? You playing fetch for him?"

Talin bristles but says nothing. I sigh. Nothing puts me in a worse mood than listening to my father drone on about what a shitty heir I am, but it's always worse if I keep him waiting. He has a wicked temper.

Kind of like me.

My father, the King of Farcliff, is sitting in the breakfast room.

Yes, we have a breakfast room.

He's sipping an espresso and doesn't lift his eyes from his newspaper as I step into the room. I stand there for a few seconds as my frustration mounts.

"Good morning, Father," I finally say.

"Charles," he says, deigning to look up at me. "How nice of you to join me. Coffee?"

"I'm going for a run. If I have coffee now, I'll shit my pants in the woods."

The King grimaces. "Do you have to speak like that? You're a prince, for crying out loud."

"Well, shitting my pants isn't very princely, either."

My father huffs, bringing his fingers to his temples and taking a deep breath to compose himself. "The Prince's Ball is coming up this weekend. You *will* be there."

I roll my eyes. "I'd planned on being in Mauritius, actually. The jet is arranged for tomorrow." I haven't actually planned that, but I like seeing my father's face turn that funny shade of purple.

Besides, if I did want to go to Mauritius, a private jet can be arranged—that's not a problem. It sounds a hell of a lot more fun than some stuffy birthday party that I never even asked for.

"Stop fucking around, Charlie!" My father slams his palm on the table. His cup jiggles in its saucer and I arch an eyebrow.

"That's not very kingly language, Father."

I know I shouldn't taunt him like that—I'm a grown man —but he and I have history, and getting under his skin is one of life's little pleasures that I find simply irresistible. His jowls tremble and a little tickle of enjoyment passes through me.

I love it, but I also know when to stop.

"Yes, your Majesty, I'm going to the stupid ball, but I'm not coming out of it with a wife."

"Charles, it's time. The laws dictate that—"

"I say when it's time," I interrupt. "I'm not getting married."

"You're the heir to the throne. You need to think about your responsibilities, and not just which girl will spread her legs for you next. If your mother were still alive…"

"Don't speak about my mother." My voice has a dangerous edge to it. My father stares me down as only a King can, and I hate that I avert my eyes before he does. I turn to leave when he stops me.

"Charles, one more thing." My father pushes the newspaper he'd been reading across the table. It slides over the polished surface and stops right in front of me. "No more boxing."

"Excuse me?"

I drop my eyes to read the headline:

PRINCE CHARLIE DELIVERS KNOCK-OUT BLOW

"What's wrong with this? I won the fight. You should be proud of me."

My father inhales, staring at me as if I'm the densest person to walk the earth. Only the King has the ability to make me feel like a child every time I'm with him.

Finally, he speaks. He talks slowly, enunciating every syllable. "You can't beat up your subjects, Charles. It's just not done." He touches his finger to the table with every word. "No. More. Boxing."

I ball my hands into fists but say nothing. Turning on my heels, I head out of the doorway. The instant I'm outside, I start running. I have to get out of that room, out of that castle. Hell, if I could leave this stupid Kingdom, I would.

My feet pound the pavement until I duck into the forest and make my way to the lake trail. Once I'm under the trees, I breathe a little deeper. The smell of fresh pine, moss, and rich soil fills my nostrils. I settle into an easy jog as the trees thin around me and Lake Farcliff appears. The water looks cold, but its gentle lapping on the shore settles my nerves.

My father has hated me ever since my mother passed away. I know he blames me for it, even though he'd never say it out loud. He hates the fact that I'm his successor—and, to be honest, so do I. I never asked for this.

Movement on the lake's surface makes me glance over.

A woman is gliding along in a boat, parallel to the trail I'm running on. She's too far away to make out the details of her face, but I watch her move through the water like poetry in motion. She's rowing at a leisurely pace, sweeping her oars over the rippling surface as if she were born to do it. She hasn't seen me, but I match her pace as I run along the shore.

Then, I speed up the tiniest bit and I smile when I see her head turn my way. She pulls the oars through the water with a little more strength, first matching my pace and then moving ahead of me. My smile widens.

So, she's like me. She doesn't like to lose.

I speed up, nosing in front of her as my feet pound the hard-packed earth.

I can't help it.

I know I'll never win. I'm not an idiot—no matter what my father likes to say. This woman was obviously resting before, and there's no way I could outrun a professional sculler in a racing boat.

But it doesn't matter. Adrenaline floods my veins at the promise of competition, and I give it all I've got. She makes another powerful stroke.

I'd like to give her a powerful stroke.

I'm in a full-on sprint now, but I already know I've lost. The young woman doesn't even look like she's trying, and yet she glides ahead of me. Before my lungs explode in my chest and my muscles spasm uncontrollably, I slow down. I lift my hand to her in surrender, and I think I see her smile.

I finally stop running and try to catch my breath. Bending over, I rest my hands on my knees. The woman slides out of view and I gulp down another breath. My heart thumps harder than it has in weeks. I laugh to myself, alone in the woods, intertwining my fingers on top of my head and inhaling deeply.

That was fun. I want to do it again.

How sad is my life that I can buy anything I want, go anywhere I wish... but my biggest thrill is losing a footrace I never could have won in the first place?

3

ELLE

"WHAT WAS THAT ABOUT? You were supposed to be cooling down," Coach Bernard grumbles as I make it back to the pier.

I decide not to answer. *I was racing some runner on the shore* just doesn't seem like something Coach would like to hear two months before the biggest regatta of the year.

It's the first time I've qualified for the Spring Regatta. As a single sculler, my event is one of the most highly anticipated ones.

Farcliff is a Kingdom nestled between the United States and Canada, near the Great Lakes. We're much smaller than either of our neighbors, with a population of under twenty million packed into a country the size of Vermont—but we're fierce. The Spring Regatta brings in all the nearby colleges, including Princeton and McGill.

The entire royal family attends the Spring Regatta, and the winners get their medals presented by the King himself. American schools have won the singles event for the past six years, and Coach Bernard thinks I could be the one to bring the trophy back to Farcliff.

Winning that event would not only mean I get to keep my

scholarship, but it also has a healthy prize purse attached to it as well. It's basically the pinnacle of any Farcliff athlete's rowing career in one event.

So, yeah—I probably shouldn't be deviating from my training to race some runner when I'm supposed to be cooling down, but I have a competitive streak and sometimes I can't help myself.

Coach Bernard is still staring at me with those assessing eyes of his, waiting for me to answer his question. Instead, I just haul myself out of the water. My coach gives me a few notes and then heads back to the athletic building. I'm almost finished getting my shell out of the water when I see movement on the shoreline.

I look up just in time to see Olivia dangling my running shoes from the tips of her fingers. A cruel grin spreads over her glossy lips.

"Oops," she mouths as she tosses them in the water.

"Hey! What the hell!" My feet pound on the pier and I make a quick turn, splashing through the shallows to grab my now-soaked shoes. I turn just in time to see her sniggering as she walks away.

"Real mature, Olivia," I call out after her. She flips me off without looking back.

Glancing at the gravel-filled pathway back up to the athletic building, I let out a sigh and swap my boat shoes for my sopping wet runners. I squelch my way up to put my scull away, and then squelch some more all the way back to the locker room.

I can hear the other girls in the locker room showers, so I just grab my stuff and leave. By the time I get to my house, hot tears are stinging my eyes.

I'm cold, wet, tired, and hungry—and perhaps most pathetically of all, my feelings are hurt. As soon as I got off the water, it only took Olivia half a second to remind me that I don't belong here. That I'm an outsider. That I'll never be one of the elite.

That I didn't get invited to their stupid, archaic Prince's Ball.

Not that I care, anyway. I wouldn't have anything to wear, and Coach has us on a strict curfew until the regatta. Going to some party would be a distraction that I really don't need right now.

It still hurts, though.

I cry in the shower, standing under the hot stream of water until I can get a hold of myself again. By the time I've toweled off, I have so much pent-up energy inside me and nowhere to unleash it. I take a deep breath. I know what I need to do.

I stomp from the bathroom to the hall closet and grab my toolbox. In four strides, I'm in front of Dahlia's door, banging on it as hard as I can. The door shakes so hard it nearly comes off its hinges.

"Dahlia!"

"Come in," her sleepy voice says.

I burst through the door like a woman possessed. "Up." I order. "Out of bed."

Dahlia frowns, rubbing her eyes with her fists. Her shoulder-length hair is dyed a multitude of pastel colors from pale pink to purple to blue, and it's splayed out across her pillow like a unicorn-colored halo.

"How was practice?" She asks, rubbing her eyes.

"It was fine." I say. "Get up."

She yawns, and my frustration mounts. My roommate throws her blankets off and stands up, completely naked. I blush, averting my eyes, but Dahlia doesn't seem to care. She glides over to the chair in the corner of the room and throws her sparkly purple housecoat over her shoulders.

"What are you doing?" She asks, cocking her head to the side.

"I'm fixing your stupid bed. Where's your friend the moaner from last night?"

She waves a hand dismissively. "He had to leave."

"You kicked him out?" I pull the bed away from the wall and glance at my roommate.

She grins. "I told him I had an early class."

"I wish I had your nerve, Dahlia." I open the toolbox and find a screwdriver. "I can't do one-night stands."

"It's easy. You just find someone you think is attractive, have sex, and then you say: 'I have an early class in the morning, so...' and leave it hanging for them to fill in the blanks." Dahlia sits down on the chair and leans her elbow on the armrest, her head propped on her palm. "They always understand."

I snort. "I get the concept of a one-night stand, Dahl. What I'm saying is I don't think I could do it. I need... I don't know. More of a connection."

"There are different kinds of connections. Sometimes, a connection lasts an instant, like a glance at a stranger on a subway. Sometimes it lasts a night. For some people—the lucky ones—they find someone to share a connection with for a lifetime."

"You really think that's true?" I tighten the screws on her headboard and then flip the heavy mattress off to check the frame underneath. "I think that only happens in fairytales."

I don't mean to sound as bitter as I do, I swear. But I never knew my parents, and I guess they must have had a connection for at least a night. Long enough to create me. I grew up in the system, ferried from foster home to foster home, enduring all types of horrors until I was fourteen. That's when I found the Valencias, who introduced me to crew. Once I found the Valencias and rowing, everything got a little easier.

Not *easy,* per se—but definitely easier.

Before that? I don't even want to think about it. My childhood is a blur that I'd rather not bring into focus.

"The only people I know who had a lifelong connection were the Valencias," I say. "That's two people out of, what? The thousands that I've met? Out of everyone, only two people have a real connection?"

Dahlia smiles that impish little smile of hers and shrugs. "Like I said, they're the lucky ones."

I tighten everything on Dahlia's bed frame and grab a plank of wood from the closet, long enough to jam across her frame to stiffen it up a little more. It's seriously Macgyvered, but at least it doesn't squeak anymore when I test it.

"Help me with this," I say. "We're moving your bed to the other wall."

"Don't I get a say in this?" Dahlia asks with a grin, even as she's getting up to help. "It's my room."

"As much as I love listening to a sex-fest every night, the Spring Regatta is coming up, and I need to sleep." We drag her frame across the room, and I help her put the mattress back on and re-make the bed. I take care not to touch her sheets too much—who knows what kind of bodily fluids are on there?

When I grab her bedside table to carry it over, a silver envelope falls to the ground. My eyes widen as I pick it up.

"The Prince's Ball?" I look up with wide eyes. How did she get an invitation?

Dahlia's naked again, hands on her hips, staring into her

closet. She glances over her shoulder at me and shrugs. "Yeah, what about it?"

"How did you get an invite?"

"In the mail," she replies, pulling on a pair of teal jeans followed by a purple sweater. It matches her hair and it makes her look completely colorblind, but the outfit still kind of works.

I take a deep breath. I love this girl to death, but sometimes she is seriously off her rocker. "I know you got it in the mail, Dahl—but why did *you* get one? I thought it was only the upper echelons of Farcliff society that got one of these."

I follow her to the kitchen as she waves a hand. "My parents know the royal family. It's not a big deal."

I frown. "Not a big deal? You told me you were putting yourself through college without their help. That's why you work at the restaurant, remember? Where we met?"

"Coffee?" Dahlia asks, smiling.

I take a breath to calm myself as my friend does her best to ignore my questions.

"Who even are you, Dahlia?" I look down at the envelope in my hands and my eyes widen. "Dahlia *Raventhal*? You didn't tell me you were a Raventhal. The same Raventhals that got kicked out of the Kingdom when the Queen died?"

I follow Dahlia into the kitchen as she hums to herself and rummages through our cupboards.

"Dahlia?" I say softly.

Finally, she leans her hands on the counter and takes a breath. "Yes, I'm a Raventhal." Then, her face brightens and she turns toward me. She puts her hands out and jumps up and down in excitement.

"What?" I ask.

"This is *perfect!*"

"What's perfect?"

"You! Elle! You're perfect!"

"What are you talking about, Dahlia?"

"You can go to the Prince's Ball instead of me. You can take my invitation and they'll tick my name off the list. My family will think I went, and it'll keep them happy. You'll get a night off to enjoy yourself, which you desperately need. It's the perfect plan!"

"Perfect is not the word I'd use to describe the nonsense that just came out of your mouth, Dahlia."

Her smile doesn't slip. She does a little dance and throws her arms around me. "Amazing! I can do your hair and makeup, and we'll find something for you to wear."

"No."

"You'll go, dance, feel pretty, and forget about whatever it is that makes you cry in the shower." Her smile widens and she hugs me again.

I freeze. She heard that?

I disentangle myself from Dahlia's arms and shake my head. "No, Dahl. Absolutely not. This is not happening. I'm not going to some stupid party by myself just because you want your name ticked off the list. And in case you haven't noticed, I'm almost six feet tall and you're barely four foot nine. I weigh about sixty pounds more than you do. No one will ever, *ever* believe that I'm you."

She waves a hand. "None of them know what I look like."

"No." I cross my arms over my chest.

Her smile drops, and her eyebrows draw together. A pain passes through my chest. Dahlia is the only constant source of positivity in my life, and I hate hurting her. She knows how hard it is to be a scholarship student, and how hard I work for my place on the rowing team.

She also knows how the other girls love to torture me. I bite my lip.

"Olivia and Marielle are going," I say softly. "I can't go. The last thing I want to do is run into them while I'm pretending to be someone I'm not."

Dahlia makes a soft noise as she sighs. She crosses her arms and drums her fingers against her bicep. Finally, she shrugs. "They'll be stuck to Prince Charlie like glue, if I know anything about them. All you have to do is avoid the Prince, and then you'll be in the clear. There'll be at least five hundred guests there. You can easily melt into the crowd."

"Look at me," I scoff, spreading my arms. "Melting into crowds isn't exactly my forte. I'm not going, Dahlia."

"I can drive you."

"You want me to pull up to the biggest event in Farcliff in your bright, orange Jeep? Whatever happened to 'melting into the crowd'? Everyone will be arriving in limousines! Listen to yourself, Dahlia—this is insane! I won't go."

"Uh-huh," she says as her face brightens again. "Coffee?"

4

CHARLIE

MY FATHER MAY BE the King, but he can't stop me living my life—and that includes boxing. I run straight from the lake trail to the gym, arriving at the old warehouse-style boxing gym soaked with sweat and hyped-up on adrenaline.

I glance further down the street, where the houses get smaller and the lawns are overgrown. Grimdale. Behind me, manicured lawns get bigger and bigger, leading to the McMansions that line the streets all the way to the castle gates.

Farcliff Kingdom is severed almost perfectly in two between Grimdale and Farcliff. Grimdale is often seen as the lower-class end of town. The residents are lower-income, working-class people. My father often dismisses them, even though they're just as much his subjects as the richer residents of Farcliff.

Money talks, though, right?

It talks to him, that's for sure.

My mother wasn't like that. She volunteered at many Grimdale organizations and was beloved by everyone. Sometimes I think my father was jealous of her—the people never cared for him like that. He doesn't have the sparkle she had, or her ability to make everyone feel loved, important, and heard.

In a way, I've tried to follow in her footsteps. I'm not perfect—not by a long shot—but at least I still respect everyone in Farcliff Kingdom. That includes the people of Grimdale

The boxing gym sits almost exactly between the two districts, like an impartial observer to both sides of the tracks. I walk inside the old warehouse, ripping my tee-shirt off and pointing to the guy pounding the bags.

"Jimmy. You and me. We're sparring. Now."

He glances from my face to my tattooed chest, his eyes widening. Then, he glances over his shoulder and shakes his head. "I'm sorry, Your Highness, I can't, I..."

"You what? You can. You've beat my ass a dozen times when I first started. Are you scared I'm going to beat you this time?" I flex my arms and he puts his hands up.

"No, I..."

"I am commanding you, as your Prince, to get in that fucking ring and spar with me."

He turns mute.

"Charlie!"

I turn around to see old Bo 'The Badger' Smith walking out of the office. He's old and hobbled now, but I've seen grainy videos of his fights. He went toe-to-toe with the best, before he started this boxing gym. Only Bo, my brothers, and a couple of other trusted people call me Charlie.

My mother used to call me Charlie, but she's gone now.

To everybody else, I'm 'Your Highness'. I've tried to get Neville to call me anything other than that, but he's a stickler for etiquette.

Bo looks at me, shaking his head. "I'm sorry, son." His eyes are soft and sympathetic.

"About what?" I pound a fist into the palm of my other hand. I need to get rid of some of this energy. I need to punch something.

Bo sighs, putting a gnarled hand to his forehead.

My heart starts to thump. "About *what*, Bo? What are you sorry about?"

"I've received a Royal Decree. If you train here, I'll get shut down." He sighs. "I'm sorry, Charlie. I tried to fight it."

White-hot rage spikes my blood. "A Royal Decree," I repeat, even though I heard him just fine the first time. This stinks of my father. I take a trembling breath. "I can't even train here? What if I don't fight? I'll just train, nothing more. I won't even spar."

Bo reaches into his breast pocket and pulls out a folded piece of paper. I take it, immediately recognizing the thick, watermarked and heavily scented paper stationary used for all royal correspondence. I wrinkle my nose as I read the decree, my heart sinking to my stomach.

If I'm caught here, Bo gets shut down.

I try to keep my face steady as I hand the paper back to Bo, but I can feel my eye twitching.

I need this gym. Ever since I was ten years old, I've been boxing. My mother brought me here when I started acting out. When the big scandal happened, back when I was fifteen —the one that damaged my relationship with my father beyond repair—boxing became my lifeline. I need the bags. I need the pain. I need Bo.

"I'm sorry, son," Bo repeats over and over again, finally putting a hand on my arm. "You know how many kids stay out of trouble because they come here. If I get shut down..."

I shake my head. "You're not getting shut down. I won't let it happen."

His eyebrows arch and I see the sorrow in his eyes. My heart squeezes in a way I'm not used to... so instead of anguish, I turn the feeling into anger. Bo has been there for me ever since I was ten years old, and now he's being threatened because of it.

It's not fucking right. I don't give a shit about being 'princely'. My father is a power-hungry, reputation-seeking, unscrupulous little man, and I will not fucking have it.

I don't even say goodbye to Bo. There's a ringing in my ears as I make my way back to the castle, my rage carrying me all the way up the wide steps to the front entrance and through the Great Hall to the King of Farcliff's personal offices. I'm ten feet away from the door when I feel a hand on my arm.

I spin around, fists raised, ready to punch the head off whoever dared to fucking touch me. My heart is pumping hot, molten lava through my veins. My eyes bulge.

"Whoa!" My brother Damon says as he throws his palms up toward me. "Easy."

I lower my fists and turn away from him. "I'm going to kill him."

"Charlie..."

I don't answer, just keep stomping to my father's office. The ringing in my ears gets louder as I see visions of my fist connecting with his pudgy, royal face. I see myself smashing him against that stupid cherrywood desk of his, and flinging him against his Persian rugs.

"Charlie!"

I spin around. "What?"

"Don't. Whatever you're going to do, don't do it."

"He's a tyrant, Damon."

"You're going to be King."

"I don't want to be King!"

"Neither do I." Damon's eyes widen and in a flash, I understand what he's saying. If I go in there and bash my father's face in, I'll be thrown out. Banished. Disowned.

I'll lose my claim to the throne—not that I care—but that means that Damon will be next in the line of succession. And Damon is no King, nor is our younger brother, Gabriel.

They haven't had the training that I've had. Ever since I was born, I've been pushed toward this. They haven't.

Don't get me wrong, Damon is strong as an ox and he has a heart of gold, but he's not made for state dinners and royal duties. He'd rather be on his own, far away from it all, nose buried in his books to study medicine. He's going to be a fucking brilliant surgeon one day—something that requires more brains than I've got.

Becoming King would sap his spirit until it killed him. As much as I despise my father, I love my brothers more. I know that neither of them is suited for the Crown. The weight of it would snap their necks.

Damon is the least confrontational person I've ever met. I don't want to put him in a position to have to deal with the Crown... and a part of me doesn't trust that he'd be able to stand up to my father. If there were important political decisions to be made, I'm the only one who could face off against my father and win.

And based on how things are going in Farcliff—with Grimdale residents becoming more and more destitute while my father consolidates power for himself—it's time for a change

It has to be me.

Which means I have to play by the rules. I have to do what I'm supposed to, like go to this stupid Prince's Ball.

For now.

My shoulders slump and I nod at Damon. "Okay."

He breathes a sigh of relief. "Thanks, Charlie." Damon points over his shoulder. "I have to go. I've got class."

I nod. "See you later. Thanks for stopping me."

"Anytime. And Charlie?"

I look up, arching an eyebrow.

"Thank you."

I grunt and watch Damon walk away. Glancing back at the door behind me, I think I see movement out of the corner of my eye. When I look again, there's nothing there.

I shake my head and walk to the garages to grab my motorcycle. The engine purrs underneath me and I take off, needing to put as much space between the murderous rage mounting inside me and the target of said rage—my father.

So, I go to the only place I know where I'll be treated like a normal human being. I weave through the streets, loving the roar of the bike underneath me as I make my way to Grimdale, to a small side road with a few shops and an abandoned building. I park my bike outside the Grimdale Animal Shelter and pull my helmet off.

When I walk in the door, Francis is standing behind the counter. He smiles at me with a deep nod. "Your Highness."

"For the love of Farcliff, Francis, call me Charlie. How many times do I have to say it?"

"Ah, but riling you up is so much more fun," he winks. I lay my bike helmet on the counter and arch an eyebrow. He shakes his head. "Your temper will be your undoing, Charlie."

"Yeah? What else is new?"

Francis grins at me and nods to the door marked 'Staff Only'. "We had a couple of strays dropped off today. I could use your help with them."

I follow him into the back, reaching into my motorcycle jacket pocket and pulling out a couple of dog treats I keep stashed there. When Francis isn't looking, I slip the treats to my two favorite dogs as they rest in their kennels. They munch happily, and Francis glances back at me.

I know he knows I feed them, but he pretends not to notice. Just another reason I like the man.

At least my father can't take this away from me. No one knows about this place—not even Damon, or Gabriel, or Neville. This is my last refuge, and the only place where I can untangle the mess that is my life.

I need to figure out how to get out from under my father's thumb. The law states that the Crown Prince must declare a bride before his twenty-sixth birthday, and tradition says that the Prince's Ball—my twenty-fifth birthday—is the event where it all gets decided.

Only once I declare a bride can my father officially name me as his heir, and the transfer of power can begin.

I think it's a load of horseshit, but my father obviously disagrees. It's a stupid tradition, anyway, one my father could change it at the drop of a hat if he wanted to.

But he doesn't.

The fact that he's pushing me to find a wife gives me pause. There's something else going on, but I don't know what it is yet. I don't trust my father with anything, least of all with my life. If he's pushing me to find a wife, it's because he's getting something out of it, too.

As Francis gives me instructions to clean out a few cages and help him with some heavy lifting, my mind drifts. Ever since my mother's death when I was eleven, my father has become a cruel man. I was the one who found her, cold and stiff in her own bed, and I think a part of him has always blamed me. No one ever discovered why she died, but my father always looked at me differently afterward.

Then, when the scandal with my governess happened, when I was fifteen—that's when things between my father and I really went south. According to him, I was tarnishing the Farcliff name and I wasn't fit to be King. He's never supported my claim to the throne, but that's one law he can't change.

If I don't find a wife, though, it would be an easy excuse for him to refuse to name me his heir—so why is he so keen to see me married all of a sudden? Seems to me it would be better for him if I *didn't* find a wife.

"Charlie, pay attention." Francis sighs as a bag of dog food drops in front of me and splits open on the floor. Kibble tumbles everywhere, causing a frenzy of activity in all the kennels that surround us. Half a dozen dogs bark excitedly at the smell of food.

My mind snaps back to the present and I lift my palms up. "My bad, Francis. I'll clean it up."

"I know you will. And when you're done, you'll give that little monster a bath." He points to one of the new dogs. "Get to work, Your Highness."

I grin, nodding. I'd knock anybody else to the ground for speaking to me like that, but Francis is like Bo—he understands me, and he gives me a refuge from being a prince. And right now, that's exactly what I need in order to figure out what's going on with my father.

5

ELLE

OLIVIA HEAPS her dirty workout clothes into my bag after our evening practice, and then bats her eyelashes at me and laughs. "Oh, I'm sorry, Elle. I thought you were my maid. My bad."

Marielle laughs, as do a couple of the other girls on the team. I brush it off. I always brush it off. I'm just here to row and get a degree from the best college in the Kingdom. After that, nothing else matters.

Just one more year.

I'm not here to go to the Prince's Ball or brush shoulders with the supposed 'elite'. I totally understand why Dahlia didn't tell me she was part of this world. If my parents were well-connected, I'd probably hide it, too.

This week has dragged on, hour by hour, and all I've heard about is the stupid Prince's Ball. Even Dahlia is under some kind of spell, talking about how she'll do my hair and what I should wear. When I tell her I'm not going, she doesn't seem to hear me.

The only remotely enjoyable events during the week are my now-daily races with the stranger on the lakeshore. Every day now, at the same time, he appears between the trees and lifts up a hand in salute. I'm always on my last lap, and my heart beats a little harder.

I always win, but it doesn't matter.

I've never been closer than a hundred feet from him, never close enough to see his face, but this week, I feel more of a connection with him than I do with anyone else in my life.

At least he's not talking about the Prince's Ball. He just wants to run, and I just want to row. We understand each other.

ON WEDNESDAY, Dahlia invites our friend Justine over to do a trial run of my hair and makeup for the Prince's Ball.

As if it's my freaking wedding, or something.

As if I'm actually going to go.

I let them, because it feels good to be around girls who aren't cruel. It's nice to have company that isn't related to rowing, and once in a while I like feeling like a girl.

"Your hair is growing so fast, Elle," Justine says to me. "Are you taking biotin supplements?"

"It is *not* growing fast. I chopped it off ten months ago and it has barely grown past my ears." Ten months ago, I got a pixie cut and regretted it immediately. For a tall, athletic woman, having a short haircut makes me feel even less womanly than I already do.

"I still think you look amazing with short hair. I don't get why you're growing it out," Dahlia says, sipping a glass of wine. She holds the stem between delicate fingers.

"Amazing?" I scoff. "I look like a man."

"Oh my goodness," she says, pushing herself out of her chair and putting her glass down. She turns my head toward the mirror and runs her hands over different parts of my face. "Razor-sharp cheekbones worthy of the cover of Vogue. Angelina Jolie lips. Big, lose-yourself-in-them-forever-and-never-look-away chocolate brown eyes. Massive tits. Girl, you are the sexiest woman in Farcliff."

My heart warms, but I just shrug in response. I stare at myself in the mirror and I try to see what she sees. Justine sweeps my hair to the side and pins it back in a special kind of way, and my heart skips. Maybe I'm prettier than I thought?

Or maybe not. I just shake my head and turn away from the mirror.

I'm not going to go to the Prince's Ball. I know I'm not. There's no point. What fun is it to go to a stuffy party where you only know a couple people—people who you happen to despise? I've listened to Olivia, Marielle, and the rest of the team talk about their nails, and their hair, and how much they spent on their outfits and as always, it just makes me feel like I don't belong.

I just want it to be over. Then, we can all focus on the Spring Regatta and I can do something I'm actually good at. If I win my event, the prize money will be enough to see me through until next year.

I'm just here to row.

ON SATURDAY MORNING, after practice, Coach Bernard gathers us all together. "Now, tonight is the Prince's Ball. I know you're all excited, so I've decided to give you the evening off. Practice is cancelled."

My tired muscles groan in relief. I might even get some real sleep tonight.

But then Coach swings his eyes toward me.

"Except you, Elle. As I understand, you're not going to the Prince's Ball, so we'll have practice as usual. That's all, you're dismissed."

Cruel laughs sprinkle around the team and my cheeks turn bright red. My heart cracks, as if a fault line appears through the middle of it, deep and jagged and unfixable.

Even my coach, who usually treats me exactly the same as everyone else, thinks I'm not worthy of the Prince's Ball. That I'm not good enough. That there's no possible way I'd ever be invited to such a fucking 'classy' event. That someone from Grimdale wouldn't have anything better to do than to practice when everyone else is trying to fuck the Prince.

Hurt turns to defiance and I lift my chin. "I'm busy, actually."

Coach Bernard swings around and stares at me. "Excuse me?"

"I said I'm busy. I thought practice was cancelled for everyone, so I made plans."

We stare at each other, and he finally dips his chin in a nod. "Just this once. And remember, ladies, curfew is still twelve o'clock. I'll have eyes at that ball and if I see any of you there past midnight, you're not racing the regatta."

A collective groan rises up. "Coach! It's the Prince's Ball!"

"Exactly—which is why I've extended the curfew from ten o'clock to twelve. Enjoy yourselves tonight." He walks out of the locker room with the assistant coaches, and Olivia immediately turns to me.

"Plans?" Olivia asks with a raised eyebrow. "What are you going to do? Have lesbo sex with your weirdo roommate all night?"

"You read my mind, Olivia," I say with an overly sweet smile, rage and adrenaline and defiance still making my whole body tense, "and I'll enjoy every minute of it."

The shock on her face is something I'll relish forever.

I grab my things and stomp out of the locker room. It's not her words that bother me. People think calling me gay is an insult—it's not.

What bothers me is that those words are trying to strip away my femininity. I know I'm not willowy and petite with waist-length blonde hair, but that doesn't make me any less of a woman.

This time, I don't cry on my way home. I'm mad, but instead of making me a weak blubbering mess, it's making me stronger. I throw my bags down as soon as I walk in the front door of my house.

"Dahlia!" I call out. "Make me into a pretty princess, because I'm going to this stupid ball."

She squeals so loudly I think I've interrupted another sex marathon, but she comes rushing out of the kitchen and wraps me in a bear hug. "I knew it! Come here."

My best friend grabs my hand and drags me into her bedroom, where I see bags and bags of online shopping deliveries.

"I took the liberty of ordering a few options. Now, your shoulders are a little bit broader, so I stayed away from anything with a high-neck or a halter top. I was thinking this off-the-shoulder number. It has a really deep neckline that I think would make the girls look *amazing*." Dahlia cups my boobs before I can smack her hand away, laughing. "Here," she says. "Try this one on first."

By the time I've tried on all the dresses she's bought— seems like hundreds of them, but it's probably closer to a couple of dozen—I'm a sweaty mess. Then, the doorbell rings and Justine walks in without waiting for us to answer. She's dragging a big suitcase. "I brought hair and makeup!"

37

With tears in my eyes, I wrap my two friends in a crushing hug. "Thank you," I sniffle.

"Go take a shower," Dahlia orders. "We'll get set up. I think I know which dress you should wear. This sequined white dress has such a gorgeous blueish shift to it. When you move, you'll look like a goddess. It also makes your body look *insane*. That's the one, definitely."

I smile. For once, I believe them when they tell me I look pretty.

I take my time showering, shaving *everything*, soaping myself up and washing my hair meticulously. Even though Olivia was cruel today, I don't cry in the shower. My heart is soaring.

I might not be accepted by the Olivias and the Marielles of the world, but I've found a few special people who love me for who I am. And I'll be damned if I let any pretentious, fake-royal, wannabe princesses dim the light that shines inside me.

6
———

CHARLIE

"WHAT DO YOU THINK, Nev? Black tie or no tie?"

Neville looks at my reflection in the mirror. "I think, Your Highness, that having no tie would suit you best."

"And it will probably piss my father off. Good choice, Nev."

I see the hint of a smile on his face before it's replaced with his usual mask of professionalism. Neville helps me put my suit jacket on and brushes lint off my shoulders. I've never worn a tuxedo in my life, and I'm not starting tonight. A black suit will have to do. I leave the top button of my shirt undone, and my chest tattoos poke out from underneath.

Straightening my jacket, I nod. "Let's go."

Before I go down to the great hall, I duck into one of the unused bedrooms and glance out of the balcony window.

Most of the guests are already here. The Great Hall opens out onto the front gardens, where tents and tables have been set up for the event. Everything is lit with hundreds of twinkling lights, and the gardeners have done a fantastic job covering every surface with flowers.

I sneeze as soon as I poke my head outside.

Lovely.

I wonder if they forgot I had allergies, or if this was another deliberate oversight from my father. Neville produces a packet of antihistamines from somewhere in his jacket.

I grin. "Always prepared, eh, Nev?"

He nods but says nothing. I look back at the crowd below, bracing myself for the next few hours of torture. My eyes dance from woman to woman, wondering which of them I should fuck tonight. They'll all be crawling all over me, so why not make the most of it? At least I can have a little fun at this torture-fest.

There's a leggy blonde in a deep red dress. She looks vaguely familiar. Brundle, maybe? She might do. She's standing with another blonde. Maybe they'd both agree to...

My eyes flick to a redhead in a black gown, and I start thinking that maybe I don't have to choose just one girl tonight. The most fuckable women in the entire Kingdom are right here, penned inside the castle walls just waiting for me to arrive. Every single one of them is desperate to take the Crown.

Well, there's another Crown they'll have to take first.

A smile slides over my lips...

...and then an orange jeep pulls up, and a woman I've never seen before climbs out. She says something to the driver and slams the door, and I know who I'll choose tonight.

I choose *her*. The goddess in the white dress, that's sparkling from across the lawn. When she moves, her dress dances around her curves. She pats her short brown hair and I let out a low groan. I fucking *love* a woman with short hair. I don't know why. Maybe it's because chicks always think they need extensions on their hair and nails and fucking eyelashes, too.

Not her, though. I hold my breath as she stops at the gates to give her invitation to the doorman.

"Nev," I say, breathless. "Find out who she is."

I see him bow out of the corner of my eye. I'm still watching her from the balcony window. She walks through the castle gate, glancing around the grounds and wringing her hands in front of her. She's nervous.

I need to get closer, but I don't want to let her out of my sight.

"Come on, girl," I say to myself, "move a little closer so I can see your face."

I *swear* she looks up at the balcony window as if she can hear me. Her hand goes to her chest, where her dress dips down between those gorgeous, plump, juicy tits of hers. I let out a sigh.

Yeah, she's the one. No question about it. Depending on how it goes, I might even call her back to the castle tomorrow.

I watch her drift to the refreshments table, right beneath my balcony, where she loads up a plate full of food. She scoops at least three spoons of guacamole onto her dish and does a little dance of excitement.

I grin. I like her more and more with every second that goes by.

All the other ladies are far away from the food. They're preening, posing, sucking their stomachs in and pushing their tits out. The only people around the food are the older guests and the men—and my mystery woman.

I know I'm too far away to hear anything, but the way she closes her eyes when she takes her first bite of food... I swear I hear her moan.

And I *need* to hear her moan. My whole body is coiled,

ready, about to be unleashed on this Amazonian goddess. Finally, I might have found a woman that can handle me. *All of me.*

I know I'll be mobbed if I go down the main steps, so I rush down the side of the building down a disused stairwell. It'll spit me out just around the corner from the caterers, and as long as she doesn't move, I should be able to talk to her without the whole Kingdom seeing me.

And if everything goes according to plan, I'll have her back in my chambers before anyone notices. And I'll drink her up and fuck her to pieces. I want her broken on my bed. I want her whimpering my name as I tear her apart. The excitement mounts inside me as I make my way to the ground floor and burst through the door.

But the one thing that makes my life simultaneously easy and completely impossible is the fact that my face is plastered all over the Kingdom. As soon as I turn the corner, all eyes turn toward me.

Including hers.

I freeze, taking her in. Taller than I thought from upstairs. Curvy as hell, with her dress nipping in at the waist in a way that makes me want to wrap my fingers around her and pull her down on top of me. Her breasts are fucking glorious. I'm rock hard the moment I lay my eyes on them, already imagining sliding my cock between them and spraying my cum all over her chest.

She's staring at me with those irresistible, brown doe eyes, with lips so soft and pink...

She licks them, and my cock throbs.

I don't know what I want to do to her first, I just know that I need her. *Now.*

"Nice of you to join us," my father says, and I jerk my gaze away from her. The King clamps his hand on my arm like a vice and drags me to the center of the grounds. I glance over my shoulder, and my goddess is still staring at me. Her eyes flash. A flush creeps up her neck, and then she looks away.

A guy puts his hand on her hip and whispers something in her ear, and she shies away from him. The instant his hand touches her perfect body, a deep, roaring well of rage start to erupt inside me. His hand is still on her waist, his lips close to her ear. I rip my arm away from my father, ready to pounce toward him and smash that smarmy jaw with a right hook.

But then she steps away from him and the pumping of my blood in my ears quiets down. My father is staring at me, wide-eyed. I clear my throat and straighten my suit jacket.

My father leads me to the center of the grounds, and all eyes turn to us. The King makes a speech, but I don't hear a word of it. The guests crowd around me and I lose sight of her, but I can't move. I'm trapped in a throng of needy guests, all clamoring for a bit of me.

I'm trapped. I just know that I'll find her again before the night is done.

Before that happens, though, I'll have to deal with all these other chicks pressing their tits against my chest and whispering desperate things in my ear. An hour ago, I would have loved it.

Well, maybe not *loved*. I would have played along.

Not now, though.

When the two blondes I spotted earlier walk up to me, one of them says, "Hey Charlie."

I snap. "That's *Your Highness* to you, girl."

Her eyes widen in shock, and then a grin curves her lips again. "I'll call you whatever you want me to call you, *Your Highness*." She bats her eyelashes at me and my stomach turns.

I need to get out of here. I need to find my goddess. But I

43

circle the grounds three times, and she's nowhere to be seen. I do laps of the Great Hall and I still don't find her. I even wait outside the restrooms for fifteen fucking minutes, but she never emerges.

She's just vanished into thin air, and I don't even know her name.

7

ELLE

Now, I understand what Dahlia was saying when she was talking about instant connections with strangers on the subway. Except, in my case, it was in the middle of the Prince's Ball that I wasn't even supposed to be attending. And the stranger on the subway? Prince. Freaking. Charlie.

The Crown Prince, and Farcliff's most notorious bad boy. The man whose face is plastered on a tabloid every weekend, who has a new girl warming his bed every night. I've seen pictures of him everywhere, but seeing him up close...

Whoa.

I'm burning up. I can't think straight. I can't even move. I stare after him, just like every other pair of eyes in this place. The only difference is, the Prince is staring right back at me.

When another man puts his hand on my hip and says something in my ear, I need to step away from him. I feel dizzy. A man has never looked at me the way the Prince just did.

Wild. Possessive.

My thong is completely drenched and my heart is beating erratically. My heels are sinking into the grass and I curse

Dahlia for convincing me to wear them. I'm already towering over everyone, I don't need heels to make it worse.

I squeeze my thighs together as heat teases between them. I'm suffocating. Everything is out of focus. Is this what a panic attack feels like?

I need air. I know I'm outside, but I need air that no one else is breathing. I need to be alone. I walk away from the food, from the party, from the King and the Prince and I head for the door that Prince Charlie just walked out of.

It's unlocked, thank goodness. As soon as I'm inside, I let out a breath. I squeeze my eyes shut and lean against the door.

Coming to the Prince's Ball was a horrendous idea. Damn Dahlia and her plans! Why did I ever listen to her?

As soon as I walked into the ball, I saw Olivia and Marielle, and the rest of the crew team. Staying away from them was easy—I just had to stand close to the food.

Everything was going to plan, until the Prince did that thing with his eyes that made me feel naked and hot and alive.

As I lean against the door, I take a deep, shuddering breath and open my eyes again. I'm in a stairwell. I should probably go back outside, but I can't face all the people there. There's way too much noise and I can't keep pretending to I know how I'm supposed to act.

Instead, I do something that I never thought I would ever do. Something that could probably get me jailed.

I take my heels off, hold them in my hands, and walk up the stairs, deeper into Farcliff Castle.

At the top of the stairs, I hesitate. I shouldn't be doing this. I shouldn't be *anywhere* here. If any of the crew team sees me, or if a castle worker sees me, or if anyone recognizes me...

46

Horror freezes my veins. Didn't Coach say he would have eyes at the party? What if I've already been seen?

I look back down the stairs and I know I can't go back there. I'll have to find another way out. Maybe if I find a different exit, I can circle back around the castle and make it home before anyone sees me.

Coming to this stupid ball was a bad, bad idea. Terrible. Why did I ever think I would belong here? How did I think this would be *fun*? This is my worst nightmare.

I push the door open and step out into a wide hallway. Doors line either side of it, and I hesitate. After a couple of seconds, this corridor is still completely silent, so I tiptoe out, as silent as a mouse. I poke my head in a room, and finding it empty, cross it to look down at the party below.

The Prince is talking to Olivia and Marielle already. My mouth tastes bitter and I turn away from the window.

Of course he's talking to them. He's going to talk to all the girls here. That's why he looked at me—he's looking for a wife.

A wife who absolutely, not in a million years, never in a million years could ever be me.

I need to get out of here. I've never belonged in a place like this, and I never should have come here. It'll end badly, I can feel it.

Finding another exit will be difficult, this place is like a maze. I make my way back into the hallway and try a couple of doors. There are more bedrooms in this castle than I ever thought possible. A few doors are locked. Most of the rooms look like they're never used.

I turn down another hallway, and then another, and pretty soon I'm completely, utterly lost.

Panic starts to set in. I start imagining one of the security guards finding me and me trying to explain how I ended up three floors above the party that I'm not even supposed to be attending. I carry my shoes and tiptoe barefoot down another hallway, ducking into a room when I hear voices around the corner. I squeeze my eyes shut, crouching against the door as if that will help me stay hidden.

Is this real life? How did I end up here?

My heart is thumping so hard I think I'm going to pass out. The voices pass the doorway without stopping and I let out a sigh. The only thing on my mind now is getting the hell out of Farcliff Castle.

I open my eyes and see that I'm in a home gym. Well, not exactly a 'home gym', since it's stocked better than our varsity college gym, but still—it's a gym.

My shoulders relax and I let my heels drop to the floor. I take a deep breath, inhaling the scent of rubber and steel and cleaning products. Unlike the varsity gym, this one doesn't smell like the stench of twenty-thousand sweaty college kids.

It feels familiar to be in here, so I take a moment to relax. No one is going to come and work out while the Prince's Ball is in full swing, so maybe I can take a moment to calm down and come up with a plan.

There's a punching bag in the corner, and I walk up to it and give it a jab. The bag is harder than I expect, and it barely moves. I punch it again, and it swings a little more. And then again, and again, unleashing all the adrenaline and fear and nerves that have been pent up inside me for the past week, the past year, the past lifetime.

"Damn, girl, what did that bag ever do to you?"

I scream, scrambling behind the punching bag as I turn toward the voice. And honest to Farcliff, it's him. It's *him*.

The Crown Prince of Farcliff, next in line for the throne, notorious bad-boy, womanizing sex god, muscled and inked like no other royal...

Yeah, that Prince. Prince Charlie.

He's here.

"You're pretty good," he says, nodding to the still-swinging punching bag as if any of this is normal. "Do you box?"

I gulp. His aura fills the whole room. It crowds around me as he takes a step closer to me, suffocating me in the sweetest, most intoxicating way. He stalks me like a predator, his steps soft and measured, his eyes low, his body coiled and ready.

Ready for what?

My breath trembles.

He tilts his head. "I know you're not mute, because you screamed when I walked in. So, I'll ask again. Do you box?"

I shake my head. "No," I manage to whisper. "No, Prince Ch—uh, Your Highness— I row."

Something flashes in his eyes and he tilts his head, and then he closes the distance between us. Sweet mother of mercy, he's *big*. Never in my life have I felt small until now. The Prince is taller than me, and wider than me, rougher than me, and more muscular than me.

And I like it—a lot.

His hand brushes my hip and sparks flash across my body. My nipples pucker and I squeeze my thighs together. I can hardly breathe as he moves even closer. His other hand touches my other hip, and he spins me slowly so I'm facing the punching bag again.

"Now," he says in a low voice that turns my insides to jelly. "Take an athletic stance. This foot forward." He taps my left thigh with his hand and I see a tattoo on his wrist poke out from under his shirt. He smells spicy and fresh and oh-so-wonderfully dangerous.

The Prince takes my arms, shaping his body behind mine as he helps me into a boxing stance. My breath becomes shallow and ragged and I'm afraid to move.

But my body betrays me. My ass presses back ever so slightly into him, and he growls. The noise rumbles deep in his chest, and he runs his fingers up the bare skin of my arms and over my shoulders.

"Who are you?" He says in my ear as his breath whispers over my skin.

"No one."

Prince Charlie chuckles, letting his hands slide over my stomach. One hand slides up between my breasts, holding my chest up so my body is fully welded against his. His fingers tease the base of my neck and my head spins. My ass rolls back against him and his breath slides over my shoulder.

He mimics my movement, pushing his hips into me and I gasp. I can feel it—*him*. He's hard, and big, and thick...

...and I've never wanted anything more.

I lean my head back against the Prince's shoulder and his thick, strong arms hold me there. I feel so secure right there, that I almost forget where I am.

Who I am.

"I'm not supposed to be here," I breathe.

"No," he says. "You're not." The hand he's holding on my chest drifts downward, under my dress to cup my breast. His fingers brush over my already-hard nipple and he pinches it between his fingers. I whimper as a zip of heat jolts down between my legs, and he does it again.

I tremble, leaning all my weight against him as he does nothing except hold me upright and tease my breast. The hand on my stomach holds me to him as his cock throbs against my ass.

Now, I know my sex life isn't much to write home about. I know I don't get out much, and I don't do one-night stands. So, I'm not exactly the most experienced person in the world.

But right now, with my body melting against the Prince's

and his hand playing with my nipple, I feel so close to orgasm that it's almost embarrassing.

Almost.

"Who are you?" He growls again, his voice more commanding this time. "Tell me."

"I can't."

He pinches my nipple *hard* and my breathe hitches. Pain and pleasure explode through me. I want more. My arm reaches back behind his head, digging my fingernails into the nape of his neck. I can't stop myself.

"Tell me your name. I command you as your Prince."

My knees quake, and my name is on the tip of my tongue. His hand on my stomach drifts down to my mound, and he presses my center back to his. The heat of his palm between my legs makes my head spin. Everything inside me is screaming to obey. Tell him who I am. Tell him anything he wants.

But I can't. No one can know I was here.

So, instead, I exhale the one word that I can still manage to say.

"No."

8

ELLE

THE PRINCE FREEZES FOR A MOMENT, but I'm so turned on I can't be afraid. He's still holding me to him, throbbing against me, teasing me and pinching me and torturing me like never before.

But then the Prince does the one things I don't want him to do. He withdraws his hand from my breast and takes a step away from me. I waver, my legs not quite ready to take my full weight again.

The Prince turns me around to face him again, tilting his head to the side. His eyes are wicked and dark. One hand stays on my hip as he brushes the other over my breast. His fingers slide up across my collarbone and then up to my lips. His hand cups my face, more gently than I'd expected from him.

"Why won't you tell me who you are?" His eyes flash. "Everyone else is dying for me to remember their name."

"I'm not everyone else."

"No," he says, running his thumb over my bottom lip. "You're not."

There are no thoughts in my head anymore. All there is

between my ears—and between my thighs—is a deep, unquenchable *want*. I want his cock inside me. I want his body pressed up against me. I want him everywhere, anywhere, anyhow.

The Prince leaves his thumb on my lips and I find myself parting them. I swirl my tongue over the tip of his thumb as he watches me. His eyes widen as a smile tugs his lips. I suck the Prince's thumb into my mouth as he watches me, the heat of his gaze making my whole body burn. When I flick my tongue over the tip of it, the tension between us heightens.

How can he do this to me? With one look, half a touch, and only a few words, I'm beside myself. Prince Charlie drags his thumb from between my lips and then crushes his mouth against them instead. My arms wrap around his neck as he backs me against the wall, caging me against it as he kisses me harder.

The Prince's tongue swipes into my mouth, dancing with mine as his hand grips the nape of my neck. I gasp, tangling my hands into his hair and pulling his face to mine. My body is on fire. He grinds his hips against me and I buck underneath him. His teeth drag across my lower lip and I make a noise at the back of my throat, nipping at him harder.

His grip on my neck tightens as he tilts my head up, kissing me more fiercely. I find the collar of his shirt and rip it open, buttons flying in all directions like confetti.

The Prince pauses, glancing down at his open shirt as a wolfish grin spreads on his lips. His eyes flash again, and he *roars*.

He wrenches my dress down to my waist and I hear it tear with a sharp, satisfying rip. The Prince cups my exposed breast with his hand as he jams his leg between my thighs. His cock is so hard it makes me ache for him. His thumb, still wet with my saliva, feels cold as he swirls it around my nipple.

He pinches it gently and chuckles when I whimper. "Are you still refusing to tell me your name?" He kisses my neck, pulling me into him and coiling his fingers into my hair.

I tremble, almost falling until the Prince pins me harder against the wall. I nod, breathless.

"I could get you thrown in jail." HIs eyes are dark as his fingers work to unzip my ruined dress. It puddles at my feet and I stand in front of him in nothing but my underwear.

"That's a risk I'm willing to take." I run my fingers over his chest, pushing his shirt off his shoulders. We stare at each other's nearly-naked bodies, devouring them with our eyes. Ink dances over his skin, rippling with every movement he makes. Prince Charlie is covered in tattoos from his neck to his waist, and I let my fingers trace his ink, his abdominal muscles, the outline of his pecs.

He's perfect.

I take a trembling breath and close my eyes for a moment. The Prince freezes, and when I open my eyes, he's staring at me curiously.

"This is new to you, isn't it?" He backs away a fraction of an inch and I miss the heat of his body. "You're not used to this."

"Not used to what?"

He runs his fingers up my sides, sending shivers through my whole body. Pressing his chest to mine, he cups my face in his hands and stares into my eyes.

"Being with a man like me."

I almost laugh. I'm not used to being with *any* men, let alone royalty.

The Prince's thumb sweeps over my lip and he kisses me again. I pull him into me, pressing my breasts against him as I grind my hips toward him. The gusset of my panties is completely drenched, and my desire for him is only mounting.

Sensing my need, Prince Charlie drops a hand between my legs and grunts when he feels my soaked underwear. His lips don't leave mine as he runs his hand up and down the outside of my panties, teasing me mercilessly as I move my hips with him.

I fumble with his pants while his lips stay locked with mine. He runs his teeth over my lip and swirls his tongue into my mouth. I moan, finally unfastening his pants and letting them drop to the ground, revealing a pair of tight, white briefs that leave nothing to the imagination. He's *big*.

My arms fly around him and we roll our hips toward each other in wild, frantic movements.

The Prince's body is insane. Everywhere I touch is hard, rippling muscle. He's chiseled from warm marble, lean and sculpted and like no one else I've ever been with. I kiss his neck, bite his shoulder, pull his hair. I need him.

And then, Prince Charlie does something that I've only dreamed of. He does something that I thought I'd never experience, that no man has ever done to me before. Something I've fantasied about, alone in my room at night, with my eyes squeezed shut and my hand between my legs.

He. Picks. Me. Up.

I yelp, fear spiking through me as my legs wrap around his waist of their own volition. He doesn't stumble, though. He doesn't drop me. He holds me as if I weigh nothing. As if I'm not almost as tall as him.

And I feel like a woman. He holds me in his arms and I feel sexier than I've ever felt before. I grind my center against him as he grunts, his cock pressed against my soaked underwear.

I curl my hands into the Prince's hair and kiss him harder, squeezing his waist between my thighs as he takes a few steps.

The energy between us crackles. Our movements are feverish as we claw at each other. He sinks his fingers into my ass as I leave long scratch marks down his back.

"Hold that," he says, nodding to a bar above me.

I don't have the energy to think—I just do what he says. I grab the bar with both hands, unwrapping my legs from his waist. He keeps his hands on my hips, teasing my neck with his lips. His hands slip my panties down over my ass. The soaking wet fabric falls to the ground and I kick it away. He gives my butt a light smack.

"Nice ass," he says, grinning.

"Thanks. I made it myself."

That gets a laugh from him, and he hooks his thumbs into his briefs and drops them to his ankles. My breath hitches, and the Prince's lips twitch into a wicked smile.

"Keep your hands on that bar. That's a command from your Prince." Without waiting for an answer, he grabs my legs and wraps them around his waist. The tip of his cock brushes against me, and I inhale.

His eyes are smoldering. I watch a vein in his neck pulse with thick, hot blood as he swallows, his Adam's apple bobbing up and down.

Then without warning, the Prince buries himself inside me to the hilt. Holding my waist, he drives his cock inside me, hard. We both grunt. I grip the bar above my head as he thrusts into me again and again, sending wave after wave of pleasure rocking through me.

Without breaking stride, the Prince grabs my legs and hooks them under his arms, spreading me even wider for him. A moan slips through my lips as his cock drives deeper inside me.

"Come for me, angel," he growls. My body is completely in his control. I hang from the bar above my head with my knees hooked over his arms as he drives himself deeper and deeper inside me. I can feel *everything*—his full length pulsing as he pushes inside me. I'm so wet it covers him completely and our bodies slap together amidst grunts and moans.

It's messy. It's rough. It's fucking incredible.

The muscles in my arms are screaming, but I don't care. I'm not letting go. The Prince takes my nipple between his lips and drags his teeth over it as he spreads me wider, punishing every part of me.

I *scream.*

My spasming is out of my control. My legs squeeze into him as an orgasm rocks through me, sending me flying over the edge as my whole body contracts around him.

The Prince lets out a moan, sucking my breast between his lips and driving himself inside me again. My body goes limp, my head lolling back with every movement of his thrusting hips.

But I don't let go.

Not until I feel his cock grow even harder. Not until I feel it push deep inside me. Not until he grunts, splashing his seed against my womb with a final, powerful thrust.

Then, finally, I let go of the bar above me—and we both tumble to the floor.

9

CHARLIE

MY MYSTERY WOMAN lands on top of me in a tangle of arms and legs. My cock slips out of her, thank fuck, otherwise the fall might have snapped it in half.

"You okay?" She props herself on her elbows. Her brows are arched in worry.

I grab her ass with both hands. "I'm great." I smack it again.

A shy smile tugs at her lips and I wonder how she could feel shy after what's just happened. "That was..." She trails off.

I grin. "It was fucking hot, that's what it was. I've always wanted to do that but I've never met a girl who was strong enough."

She smiles, blushing. I bring my lips to hers and kiss her... and then freeze. "Are you on the pill?"

She opens her mouth to answer just as the castle clock-tower starts ringing. The mystery girl's eyes widen and she jumps up off me. "What time is it?"

"Midnight," I answer, frowning. She hasn't answered my question. If she's not on the pill, she'll have to get the morning after pill. I've already learned my lesson a long time ago—I can't trust women when it comes to pregnancy. All they want is a little bastard child by me so they know they'll be set up for life.

No fucking way.

But before I can ask her again, she's pulling on her underwear and scrambling to get her dress.

"What are you doing?"

"What does it look like I'm doing?" She pulls on the tattered remains of her gown, sighing as it falls halfway down her chest. "Damn it."

"Are you leaving?"

"Yeah. I gotta go. Curfew."

"*Curfew?*"

Finally, she looks up at me. "Yes, Your Highness, curfew. I'm supposed to be home by midnight, and as it is, it doesn't look like that's going to happen. I'm not supposed to be here."

"Call me Charlie," I say, surprising myself. "Who are you?" I ask.

She runs over to me, placing a soft kiss on my lips. "Thank you for tonight. You have no idea how much it meant to me."

"Wait—"

But she's already heading for the door, holding her ruined dress up with both hands.

"Hey! You never answered. Are you on the pill, or...?"

She pauses at the door, glancing over her shoulder with a withering look. "What makes you think I'd want to get pregnant, Your Highness? Please. I have other things to worry about." She shakes her head, walking out, and a spark of shame flashes in my heart.

I stare at the door where she disappeared for a few seconds, frowning. Finally, I snap out of it and run out of my gym, sprinting halfway down the hallway. I need to know who she is. I need to see her again.

After tonight, I know I won't be able to settle for another woman. It won't be enough. Nothing will be enough until I have her again—hopefully sooner rather than later. I sprint down the hallway in one direction, and then double back and check the other exits. There's no sign of her.

Movement catches my eye, and Talin comes stalking around a corner. He arches an eyebrow, flicking his eyes down to my naked body.

"Your Highness," he says with a small bow.

"Did you see..." I trail off. The girl said she shouldn't be here, and I don't want to get her in trouble by telling Talin about her.

What did she mean by curfew? What kind of grown woman has a curfew?!

I ignore Talin and turn around, walking my naked ass back to my gym.

I'd come here for a bit of peace and quiet, thinking that no one would be in here. Well, someone was here, but *who* is still a mystery.

I pull my clothes back on item by item, mulling over what just happened. She was... incredible.

A current of frustration starts seeping through me as I think of her refusal to tell me her name. No one has ever done that. No one has ever wanted to stay anonymous from me. No one has stood up to me like that—all the while being dripping wet and begging for more.

And, like an idiot, I gave her exactly what she wanted— and without protection. Gave her what *I* wanted, too. Something came over me, and I couldn't control myself. She was so different. So special. So... perfect. I didn't even think about the consequences until it was too late.

That's not like me.

It won't happen again.

Pulling my shirt back on, I sigh as I realize every single button save for one has been ripped off. I'll have to go back to my chambers to get a new shirt before going back down to the guests. I run my fingers through my hair as I make my way to the exit.

A flash of white catches my eye.

Her shoes are lying forgotten by the door.

I pick them up, turning them over in my hands, as if they'll give me some kind of clue as to her identity. They don't. Still, for some reason, I take them with me on my way back to my rooms.

I take a shortcut through the castle and pass in front of my father's office. Voices make me pause.

"Completely naked, Your Highness," Talin says.

Snitch.

"Probably screwing some whore, no doubt," my father replies. I can imagine him waving a hand dismissively. "As long as he doesn't get anyone pregnant, I suppose it doesn't matter."

My blood turns to ice as rage flows through me. *As long as I don't get anyone pregnant?* He never loses the opportunity to remind me of the scandal that rocked my life when I was just a teenager. It's been almost a decade, now, and yet he still brings it up every chance he gets.

"If he does, it'll be his problem to deal with," Talin says. "We have the Farcliff Dam Project to deal with. The Prince knocking up half the Kingdom isn't an issue anymore."

My eyes widen and my breath catches at the sound of his voice, the anger intensifying inside me. Hatred is too kind a word for what I feel for those two. Who does Talin think he is? Why does my father let him speak about me like that?

Then I realize what else he said. The Farcliff Dam Project was rejected by the cabinet way back when my mother was still alive. She campaigned against it, because building a dam on Farcliff Lake would mean flooding all of Grimdale. Why are they talking about it now? And what the hell does it have to do with my sex life?

I lean in toward the door to hear my father sigh. "Mostly, I feel sorry for the women he chooses. Poor things."

My hand trembles as I reach for the doorknob. She wasn't a 'poor thing' tonight. She was a fucking goddess. I'm sick of my father belittling me like this. He's up to something, and all I want to do is beat it out of him.

But I remember my brother Damon's words, and I know that I can't burst in there. I can't make a scene, and I can't give my father an excuse to get rid of me.

For the sake of my brothers, I need to be on my best behavior. And as much as I hate to admit it, my father's right —that includes not knocking anyone up.

Until I know why the King all of a sudden wants me as an heir—and if this whole Farcliff Dam Project has anything to do with it—I'll have to play by his rules.

I bite my lip and turn away, gripping the mystery woman's heels in my hands as I make my way to my chambers. I place her shoes in the bottom drawer of my dresser and slam it shut.

I need to find out who she is. I need to see her again.

Flopping down on my bed, I squeeze my eyes shut as the whisper of her kiss dances across my lips. She's making my blood burn like I've never experienced before, and the thought of never finding out her name is not an option.

I *will* find her, and I will make her mine.

My lips curl into a smile when I think of her. Who knows? Maybe she's the one. My father would love that.

What if his stupid Prince's Ball does result in me finding a woman?

Not just a woman—*the* woman. The woman of my dreams.

I'm pulled from my thoughts by a knock on the door. "Come in," I say, pushing myself up to sit on the edge of the bed.

Nev walks in and gives me a small bow. His forehead is creased, and it takes him a few seconds to drag his eyes up to mine.

"Yes?"

"Sir," he sighs. "I have her name, as requested. The woman in the white dress."

My mouth goes dry and I stand up. My heart thumps and I take a step toward my butler. "Well? What is it?"

"Dahlia Raventhal," he says, and my stomach sours.

A Raventhal?

Shit.

10

ELLE

My bare feet are cut and bleeding by the time I stumble into my apartment. Dahlia pokes her head out of her bedroom door, the smile quickly slipping off her face as she takes in the sight of me. My best friend's eyes widen and horror paints itself on her features.

"Elle! What happened? Oh my gosh, are you okay?"

"I'm fine. I'm good." My lips twitch and understanding flits across Dahlia's face.

"You had sex, didn't you?"

I start laughing and clap my hand over my mouth. My torn gown falls to my waist and I scramble to pick it back up as the giggles bubble through me. Dahlia stares at me, wide-eyed with amazement. Her mouth drops open and she shakes her head.

"Well I'll be... Who was it?"

I shake my head, squeezing my eyes shut. I can't tell her. I can't tell *anyone*. That's the kind of gossip that will get me kicked off the rowing team, out of Farcliff University, and possibly even out of the Kingdom. No one can know that I slept with the Prince... including the Prince himself.

"Don't know," I say, averting my eyes. I'm a terrible liar.

But if Dahlia notices, she doesn't say anything. She just claps her hands and laughs, hopping and dancing toward me. "What happened to your dress? Your shoes? Your hair? Are you sure you weren't attacked by a pack of hungry cougars on the way home? You're a mess."

I shake my head, grinning. "No cougars. Just him. It was... intense."

"Never have I ever been more proud."

"I need a shower."

"Yes, you do," Dahlia nods. "And I'll be right here in the kitchen patiently waiting for all the details when you come out."

BY THE TIME Dahlia lets me go to bed, it's well past two o'clock in the morning. I tell her I didn't know who the guy was, despite her repeated prodding. Mostly, she seems proud of me. In a way, I'm proud of myself, too. It felt good to let go and do something crazy. My life has been so regimented and so focused on rowing that I haven't had any time to let loose.

What little hair I do have, I let down in a big way tonight.

I get to my bedroom door when Dahlia calls out. "Did you use protection?"

I freeze, slowly turning to face her. She leans against her bedroom door, eyebrow arched. "Did you?"

I shake my head.

"Elle!"

"I know, I know. We just went for it. I know it was irresponsible, but it just... happened." I shrug.

"And you're not on the pill." Dahlia's face is stern.

It's not a question—she already knows I'm not—but I still answer. "No. I started getting migraines and it was affecting

66

my rowing, so I went off it. It's not like I'm having sex regularly."

"I'll go with you to get the morning after pill tomorrow."

I bite my lip. "I can't, Dahlia. My medical records get monitored by the rowing team. If they see that I'll be in deep trouble."

"I'll get the pill in my name, and you can use it."

"This town is too small, Dahlia. Someone will find out."

"Not from me."

"If the morning after pill makes me sick, I'll miss practice and Coach will know something is wrong."

"So you can't take *one* day off rowing even if you're sick?"

"Dahlia, the Spring Regatta is in seven weeks. I can't take any days off. Tonight *was* my day off. I shouldn't have even been there! If anyone finds out, I could be benched for the regatta."

"Coach Bernard is not going to bench his best female sculler for the most important regatta of the year."

"He's done it before. Last year, he benched Maddie McLennan when she went out partying the night before practice."

"So, what? You'll risk getting pregnant? Won't that affect your rowing a *little* more than a bit of cramping from the morning after pill?" Dahlia takes a step toward me, hands on her hips and lips pinched together. I've never seen her this serious.

"We had sex *one* time. What are the chances of me getting pregnant? Almost zero."

"'Almost zero' isn't the same thing as 'actually zero'," she says, drawing her eyebrows together. "Come on, Elle. Think about this."

I pinch the bridge of my nose. That's the thing, though—I can't think. It's way past my bedtime, and tonight has been far too much to take in. Every two seconds, my mind flicks back to the Prince. To his hands on my body, his lips on mine, his...

I know she's right. I should be responsible, but the timing couldn't be worse. There's too much at stake. I can't miss practice on Monday, and I've seen how sick girls get after taking the morning after pill. I can't risk anyone knowing Dahlia got the pill for me, either. I can't risk *anyone* finding out about tonight.

The chances of me getting pregnant are so small, it seems so unlikely...

I shake my head. "Dahlia, please. I'll take my chances. There's no way I'm pregnant from one time."

"You're an idiot."

"I just want to row. If I lose that, I lose everything. You know how much that prize money would change my life and how much I need this scholarship."

My friend's forehead creases, and her pale blue eyes stare into mine. She lets out a sigh and finally nods. "I get it. I don't agree, but I get it. You're risking more by taking the pill than you are by not taking it."

My shoulders relax a fraction of an inch. I nod. "Exactly."

"Fine." Dahlia throws me another sideways glance and sighs. "At least you got to have fun tonight. Did you see Prince Charlie at all? Is he as hot as everyone says?"

Hotter. "Only from a distance," I say, glancing away. "I didn't go near him."

When I lift my eyes up to Dahlia's she's staring at me curiously. Then she shrugs. "Okay. Goodnight."

We each go into our bedrooms, and I lie in bed staring at the ceiling. I'm not ready to sleep yet. I close my eyes, committing every detail of the night to memory. I know I'll never have an experience like this again, and I want to be able to think back on it in as much vivid detail as possible.

The feel of the Prince's—of *Charlie's*—rough hands on my skin. How his tattoos shifted and slid with his skin when he moved. How his lips tasted sweet and his skin tasted sweaty, and how he smelled like pine and spice. And maybe most importantly, I remember how he made me feel.

Picking me up, driving himself inside me, grunting, looking at me like I was a goddess. I've never been looked at like that before. I've always been the ogre, the freak.

But not with him.

He made me feel like a woman. He made me love my body in a way that I've never loved it before. I've always liked what it can do, of course—that's what makes me great on the water—but I've never felt so attractive in my entire life. I squeeze my eyes shut and run my hands over my body, bringing them up to my chest.

My heart thumps under my palm, and it feels like something shifts inside me. This night is significant. Not just because of the sex, but because it makes me realize that I *am* desirable.

Before Charlie looked at me with those dark, heady eyes, I hadn't realized how much insecurity I held inside. But now...

Now, I know what I've been missing—and I want more.

I want to have that feeling with me all the time.

The only problem is I can never, ever have it again.

11

CHARLIE

I'VE BARELY SLEPT all night. I pace my room back and forth, running my fingers through my hair. Catching a glimpse of myself in the mirror, I sigh and pat my thick, dark hair back down again. I look like a mess.

After Neville told me Dahlia's name, I couldn't go back to the party.

The Raventhals were kicked out of Farcliff after my mother died. Tabitha Raventhal—Dahlia's mother—was one of my mother's best friends, and she was making a lot of noise about an inquest into my mother's death. Lady Raventhal went on the news saying the Queen had died suspiciously.

I don't remember all the details—I was young, barely eleven years old when my mother died, but I do remember it caused a lot of fuss at the castle, and Tabitha Raventhal's claims were largely ridiculed. She ended up trying to take me away from my father, and the whole thing made my mother's death that much more difficult to deal with.

My father had the entire Raventhal family removed from Farcliff. It was a disaster. I remember being angrier than I'd ever been at the Raventhals for desecrating the memory of my mother like that. I was just a kid, and I was grieving. That's probably what Tabitha was doing, too—trying to find some sense in a senseless death.

Inviting the Raventhals to the Prince's Ball has been the first olive branch since my mother died.

And now, I've just slept with her daughter? That's a bit more than an olive branch. If my father finds out, he'll think I did it to spite him. He'll think it's an insult to the Queen's memory.

I should never have had unprotected sex with her. With a *Raventhal?* How stupid could I be? I should have insisted that she tell me she was on contraception, or at least make sure she took the morning after pill. Maybe she's just here to cause more controversy, just like her mother did.

Then, I remember the way she looked at me as she was leaving. *I'm not trying to trap you. I have other things to worry about.* Her words play in my head, over and over.

She was telling the truth. She wasn't trying to have my kid. I'm just paranoid. I've always been like this—ever since the whole mess with my governess. I sit down on the edge of my bed, dropping my head in my hands and groaning. There are too many memories trying to come to the surface right now. The name Raventhal makes me think of my mother's death, and my mother's death makes me think of everything that happened in the years that followed.

After my mother died, things spiraled out of control. I don't remember much about those years. My father was angry with me often. I didn't have any friends.

Then, there was my governess, Charlotte Thorne. My first love, and my first betrayal—at the tender age of fifteen. That was the start of my locked trash cans and worries about illegitimate children.

72

So yeah, you could say I've got some baggage.

I know I have issues trusting women, and I know I'm paranoid about them using me to get pregnant, but last night felt different. A part of me wants to trust her—and that scares me.

But I knew it the moment I saw her get out of that orange Jeep—she's not like other women.

Dahlia Raventhal would probably be my father's last choice for a wife for me—if he accepted her at all.

My hair is sticking up again, and I didn't even realize I was running my hands through it. I rub my palms over my face and groan. This is a fucking mess. I'm hung up on a woman who's been banished from the Kingdom for nearly fifteen years.

If Dahlia hadn't been there last night, I could be happily waking up next to one of the countless other girls at that party whose mother hadn't caused shockwaves across the entire Kingdom. My life could be the same as it was twenty-four hours ago. Instead, I'm pacing my room like a madman as a sick feeling gurgles in my stomach.

No wonder she wouldn't tell me her name. If I'd have known, I'd never have slept with her. Instead, she took advantage of me and my stupid sex drive. My lips pinches together and distaste sours my stomach until I feel like throwing up.

The nausea curls up my spine, icing my veins and making me reach for something—anything—that will make it go away.

So, I reach for anger. I stop pacing, standing in the middle of my room as I let the memories of my past come flooding back the surface.

The shock of finding my mother dead. The grief. The horror of Tabitha Raventhal's accusations. The shame that it brought on my entire family.

The anger.

Ah, anger—I know it well. Anger thaws the ice in my veins and shields me from the shame of what happened with Charlotte Thorne. Rage twists my lips into an ugly smile and makes my eyes flash. It makes me the best boxer that Bo has ever seen. It makes me a fucking animal in bed—the kind of man that women come crawling back to even though they know they shouldn't.

Yes, anger is my friend, and I'm going to use it.

I go to my bathroom and splash some water onto my face, giving the emotion time to ripen in my blood. When I look at myself in the mirror, my eyes are dark and my face is determined.

I'm going to find Dahlia, and I'm going to make her pay.

IT'S NOT hard to find someone when you're royalty. Neville has already done the hard work, and he hands me an address as soon as I call him. It's just past nine o'clock in the morning, and it's high time I confronted Dahlia Raventhal.

The instant I get her address, I grab her forgotten shoes and go straight to my bike, tearing down the streets on my way to Dahlia's house.

A thousand thoughts cross my mind.

I wonder what she's wearing.

My grip on the bike tightens and I shake that particular thought away. That's not what I want to think about. I want to remember the pain of her mother's accusations and how they ripped my family to pieces. How the Raventhals leaving Farcliff was the best thing that could have happened.

Yes, those are useful things to think about. Not the scent of Dahlia's hair, or the way her moans made my cock throb.

Not the way I wanted her full, pink lips wrapped around my girth.

Maybe I could fuck her just one more time... I could teach her a lesson about lying to me.

My lips curl into a smile. I'll teach her a *hard* lesson. There'll be no softness in me this time. She'll be the next one with my handprint on her ass. I'll use her body and leave her behind—just like I always do. Just like it was done to me when I was too young to know what was going on.

The motorcycle roars underneath me as I accelerate. I want to be cruel. I want her to want me so badly she can't let me go... and then I'll walk out of her life forever.

No one lies to me about who they are. Because that's exactly what Dahlia did when she refused to tell me her name. She lied.

There's only one way to deal with liars. Teach them a lesson that they won't forget.

When I reach the address, I see the orange Jeep in the driveway and I know I'm here. I park my bike on the street, ripping my helmet off and leaving it on the seat. I take her shoes in my hand, letting them dangle from my fingertips as I look at the house. I leave the keys in the ignition. This won't take long.

Fuck and chuck, as they say.

Dahlia lives in a little one-story house on the far end of town, close to the border with Grimdale. It's surprising—I'd have thought her family could afford a lot more. But maybe this is part of Dahlia's sneaky, underhanded scheme to convince people that she's someone she's not.

My heart is thumping when I walk across the overgrown front lawn. I tell myself it's anger, but I know the truth.

I want to see her again.

That probably makes me weak and pathetic, but I can't

help it. I want to taste her lips again. I want to taste *all* of her. All night long, I've fended off thoughts of her sweet, silken pussy as it sucked my length inside. I've tried to ignore the throbbing, insatiable need that she awoke in me, but I can't ignore it any longer.

My fist hovers in front of the door, ready to knock it down if I need to. I take a deep breath.

One more time—that's all I'll allow myself. I'll fuck her once more, and then I'll never speak to her or her lying, despicable family again.

Then, I bring my fist to the door and pound against it. In those never-ending moments between the time I knock and the time the door opens, I don't breathe. Agonizing seconds tick by, until I finally hear light footsteps on the other side and the door swings open.

"Finally, I was wondering when you'd—" She freezes. The short, pixie-like girl at the door looks at me with wide eyes. Her jaw drops and stays hanging open.

She's wearing nothing but a t-shirt and barely-there underwear. Her hair is a thousand different pastel shades wrapped up in two high pigtails on either side of her face. She has glitter on her cheeks. Under any other circumstances, I'd have this chick in bed in fifteen seconds flat, just to see if she's as wild in the sheets as she looks.

But I'm not here for her. I'm here for Dahlia.

"I'm looking for Dahlia Raventhal."

Her mouth snaps shut, and I watch her gulp. "You found her," she says with a nervous smile, and then she does something I don't expect. Something that tells me I might have made a mistake, and that maybe the girl from last night wasn't Dahlia after all.

The girl in front of me curtsies, bowing her multi-colored head and sweeping one leg behind in a graceful movement.

Not an awkward, unpracticed curtsy. No, this looks like she's been trained to do it since the day she learned to walk. And in that moment, I realize that the girl from last night never did this. She didn't know how to act when she saw me. She wasn't even sure what to call me.

This girl, with the unicorn hair and glitter-bombed face —she knew... *This* is Dahlia Raventhal.

12

ELLE

I DIVE BEHIND a tall hedge when I see Prince Charlie at the door. The two coffees I'm holding slosh out of their cups and burn my hands, and I drop the muffins I bought onto the dirt.

"Damn it," I say, crouching down and peeking around the hedge. Dahlia looks so stunned that under any other circumstances, I'd laugh.

Except for the fact that the Prince is *at my house*. I can't laugh about that. How did he find me so quickly?

My breath grows ragged. Pretty soon, I'm on the verge of hyperventilating. Dahlia curtsies—something I've never seen her do before—and says something to the Prince.

I force myself to look at him as heat blooms between my legs. Even at a distance, he has this effect on me. I bite my lip, squeezing my thighs together and praying that he'll go away. I watch him glance behind Dahlia, his eyes squinting as he tries to see something over her shoulder.

No, not something—someone.

Me.

He's trying to find me. How did he get here? My heart thumps as panic trips up my spine. I'm already almost hyperventilating, with coffee burns on my hands and dirty muffins on the ground. I'm running on hardly any sleep, with excitement and adrenaline from last night still coursing through my veins.

What's a little panic added to the mix?

Was I followed? Does Prince Charlie know my real name? How did he find me?

And then like a flash, I know how he found me. Well, not me... Dahlia. The invitation had her name on it.

I peer around the hedge again just in time to see him turning, and I duck down, leaving the muffins behind to jump into the neighbor's yard. I sprint down the side of our neighbor's house as his motorcycle roars to life. I zip back over the fence to our yard and make it safely back inside my own house.

I put the coffees down and lean against the back door, exhaling. He didn't see me. He's gone.

"You 'only saw him from a distance'?" Dahlia says, appearing from the hallway with an arched eyebrow. Her hands are on her hips and she's shaking her head. "You 'didn't go anywhere near him'? I believe those were the exact words you used."

We stare at each other. I say nothing. What can I say? I had sex with Prince Charlie. No, not just sex. I had wild, primal, animal sex with him. He made me realize what I've been missing. He changed the way I look at myself with one mind-melting orgasm.

But based on the look on her face, Dahlia already knows this. A smile twitches over her lips and she shakes her head. "My, my, my, Elle. You are full of surprises."

"Please don't tell anyone."

"You're lucky I love you with all my heart, because this is the juiciest bit of gossip I've ever heard."

"What did you tell him?"

"I told him I was Dahlia, and I lived alone."

I breathe a sigh of relief, and Dahlia walks toward me.

"You better hope he doesn't come back, Elle. If he sees you here, he'll probably throw you over his shoulder and lock you in one of the castle towers."

"That might be all right. I don't mind the sound of that."

Dahlia grins. "Based on the expression on his face when he asked for you, looks like you made *quite* an impression." She points a thumb over her shoulder as she grabs one of the coffees. "He had your shoes, by the way."

I groan. My only pair of heels, and I left them in the castle. "Why didn't you ask for them back?"

"I live alone, remember? He took one look at my feet and saw they'd never fit me."

I glance down at Dahlia's tiny little elf feet beside my more human-sized ones. Her shoes are at least three sizes smaller than mine. "Right. I guess I'm out a pair of heels, then. Small price to pay for the best sex of my life."

Dahlia grins. "Where's my muffin?"

"I dropped it when I saw him at the door. It's behind the neighbor's front hedge."

Dahlia laughs. "You're a nutter."

"Pot, kettle...?"

"Hey, I'm not the one who banged Prince Charlie last night, fucked him so good he comes all the way to my house in Grimdale for round two, and then hid behind a bunch of bushes. That's some next-level crazy right there."

A flush warms my cheeks and I look away, shrugging. "He wasn't here for round two. Probably just here to bring my shoes back."

"Elle." Dahlia rolls her eyes. "He was here for rounds two through thirty, trust me. Why would the Prince of Farcliff return some chick's shoes unless he wanted another roll in the hay?"

My face is now bright red, even though I hear Dahlia 'rolling in the hay' multiple times a week, and I've seen her naked more times that I can count. "I have to get ready. I'm going to my parents' place for lunch today."

I haven't seen the Valencias in almost a month, and I promised I'd see them this weekend... and it's also a good excuse to get away from Dahlia's prying questions.

Dahlia just makes a tutting sound and purses her lips. "Fine. But this conversation isn't over."

"It is for me," I laugh, heading for my bedroom. Dahlia's laser-sharp eyes follow me, and I know she won't let this go. She won't tell anyone about last night—she's too good a friend for that—but even having even one other person know that I slept with the *Prince*, for Farcliff's sake... Well, that makes me nervous.

The Prince's Ball is supposedly where the eldest, unmarried son of the King finds a wife. The only people who are invited are lords and ladies and members of the social elite. You know, *suitable* brides and their families. People like Marielle and Olivia.

Not some foster kid from Grimdale. Not me.

If the Prince finds out who I really am, I'll be in deep trouble. I wasn't supposed to be at the Prince's Ball at all, and if he finds out I'm just a commoner, he'll think I lied to him.

Well, I mean, I *did* lie to him.

He could have me thrown out of Farcliff University, which would be the end of my rowing career, and the death of my reputation. If Coach Bernard or any of the team find out I was there, the consequences will be just as bad.

I can't lose my scholarship. It's the only thing I have that will give me a shot at a better life... a chance of moving beyond my Grimdale past.

No one can know I went to the Prince's Ball. *No one.*

But as I sit in my bed and sip my coffee, my thoughts drift back to the Prince. For one night, no one looked at me like a leper. No one snarled at me, or treated me like I was some sort of sub-human. I hadn't realized how much I've internalized being treated like that.

For the first time in a long time, I wish I didn't come from Grimdale. I wish I knew who my parents were, and that I'd received an invitation to the ball with my own name on it. I wish I didn't need to fight for my spot on the rowing team, even though I'm the best athlete on the team by far.

I wish I could tell the Prince my real name.

With a sigh, I lock last night into a deep corner of my heart, and I start getting ready for lunch at the Valencia's place. My parents—because Frank and Tina Valencia have been real parents to me, even though they only came into my life when I was fourteen—will want to know how my training and classes are going. They'll feed me and shower me with love, and I'll feel like I belong somewhere.

Last night is just a memory now, and even though nothing in my life has changed, I feel like I've lost something I never even had to begin with.

13

CHARLIE

I DRIVE my motorcycle around the block and park it in a side street. Then, I strip my riding jacket and helmet off, and walk back toward Dahlia's house.

The girl I met at the door *is* Dahlia Raventhal—I could tell by the way she acted around me, and by her resemblance to her mother—but I don't believe for a second that she lives alone. Why she'd live in such a dump is beyond me. The Raventhals were one of the wealthiest families in the Kingdom before they were banished, and as far as I know they've done all right after they moved to the United States. Dahlia could definitely afford a nicer place closer to the castle.

Something doesn't add up.

I put the mystery girl's shoes on my motorcycle seat and snap a picture, sending it to Neville. I follow up with a phone call.

"Nev, can you put an ad up online to find the owner of these shoes?"

"Of course, Your Highness."

"I want you to call anyone who answers the ad, and find out their name and address. Every single person."

"They didn't belong to Miss Raventhal?"

"No," I answer without further explanation. "Just put the ad out."

"No problem."

When I hang up the phone, I toss the shoes back under the seat and get on my bike. I rack my brain, trying to remember every second of my interaction with my girl.

She said she had a curfew, and she shouldn't even be at the ball. She said she liked to row. Maybe she goes to Farcliff University? I see the rowing team on the water every morning. Hell, my daily footrace is with a girl from Farcliff U. I've seen the emblem on her boat, even if she's never gotten close enough for me to see her face.

Revving the bike, I make my way to the university. I drive slowly, winding back and forth outside dorms and apartment buildings, looking for any kind of clues as to who she might be. It's pointless, though. Why would she have had Dahlia Raventhal's invitation if she didn't know Dahlia?

So, instead of going back to the castle or driving aimlessly for any longer, I make my way back to Dahlia's run-down bungalow. I park a block away and cover the rest of the distance on foot. Sneaking between two houses, I shield myself behind an overgrown shrub and the corner of a dilapidated house.

My shoes sink down in the muck, and I wait.

I don't know what I'm waiting for. I don't even know if Dahlia was lying or not, but I still stay there and wait. A neighbor takes out their trash, and a handful of cars drive by. After almost an hour, I start to lose patience.

I text Neville, asking him if he's gotten any hits on the ad yet. There are a few, he says, but he's already ruled most of them out.

This woman just disappeared into thin air.

This is stupid. I'm standing in the mud, waiting for a woman who probably doesn't even live with Dahlia. And all for what? To confront her? To demand that she tell me who she is? To fuck her again?

Maybe I just don't like being played. I'm the one who decides when a relationship is over. I'm the one who tells a woman when to leave my bed, not the other way around.

I snort at myself. My father is right about one thing—I have an ego the size of Farcliff. I can't even handle a single woman not falling to her knees in front of me and begging me to fuck her.

Maybe that's why I need to see this girl again. My fucking ego is bruised.

Shaking my head, I sigh and peel myself away from the building. I need to go home, because there's obviously no point being here. Dahlia Raventhal probably doesn't have anything to do with any of this. Who knows? Maybe she was telling the truth when she said the invitation to the Prince's Ball was lost in the mail.

But as I start to move, the front door of Dahlia's dump opens and my heart stops.

She's here.

I fucking knew it.

Heat flashes through me, and I don't know if it's anger or desire, or both. My mystery woman walks out of the house wearing jeans and a baggy t-shirt with a purse slung across her body. I watch her run her fingers through her ear-length brown hair and a shiver runs through me.

Damn, she's hot.

She turns when the door opens again, and Dahlia

appears. She says a few words to my girl, but I can't hear what they are. Then, Dahlia tosses something that glints in the sunlight. My girl catches it easily, and I realize it's the keys to the orange Jeep in the driveway.

My girl—I shouldn't be calling her that, but I can't think of her any other way—waves at Dahlia and heads for the Jeep with a smile.

Now, I'm sprinting. I make it to my bike in ten seconds flat, throwing my helmet and jacket on and straddling the seat. I crank the engine and skid around the corner just as the Jeep disappears around a bend at the other end of the street.

My heart races. I'm speeding down the residential streets, and I don't care who sees me. When I get the Jeep back in my sights, I release the throttle a bit and slow down. My mouth is dry. My pulse is hammering.

She's *right* there.

The woman who's driving me mad, who won't tell me her name, who has Dahlia Raventhal lying for her... she's in the next car.

And I want her.

I'm not even mad anymore. I don't care about the past, or about the Raventhals. I don't even care why she doesn't want me to know her name. I just need her.

I need to make her mine. I need to throw her over my shoulder and carry her back to my bed. I need to fuck her into oblivion until she screams my name.

As she makes her way deeper into the heart of Grimdale, my senses heighten. My blood runs hot, but it's only at the thought of feeling her body against mine again. She turns down a tree-lined street and I accelerate to catch up. When I turn the corner behind her, the orange Jeep is already parked outside a house.

My girl is walking up to the front door. I pause at the end

of the street, flipping my visor up and watching her. She hugs the woman who answers the door, and then disappears inside the house.

Who the hell is she?

That's the question that propels me forward. Even though every instinct is telling me to hang back, to think, to be smart about this... I need to know. I park my bike behind her Jeep and take a deep breath.

The house is tidy. It's freshly painted with a lush green lawn. It's small, but it's well-kept. I pull my helmet off and hold it in my hand as I peek inside the Jeep.

There's nothing of note in it—nothing that would tell me who this girl is. I swing my eyes back up to the house as my heart starts pumping.

I have no plan. There are no thoughts in my head except *find out who this girl is*. My feet carry me to the front door before I can stop myself, once again compelled to ring a stranger's doorbell just to find the girl I slept with last night.

This isn't me. I'm not this desperate, out-of-control, girl-crazy guy who chases after women.

Women chase after *me*.

Being here goes against everything I stand for. I *never* care. Yet, something about this girl is irresistible. She doesn't act how I expect her to. She doesn't move, or dress, or carry herself like any other woman I've met.

She's *different*.

I like her. I like her a lot more than I'm willing to admit to myself—and a lot more than I should after just an hour with her.

I'm the Prince of Farcliff, though, so fuck it. These people are my subjects, and they *will* answer the goddamn door and let me in to their house. I have nothing to hide, and nothing to fear.

I ring the doorbell again.

Any second now, I'm going to find out who my mystery woman is, and I'm going to teach her a *hard* lesson about disobeying me. When I ask her what her name is, she better answer me, or there'll be hell to pay.

I straighten my shoulders as I hear footsteps on the other side of the door. I'm ready for this. I own the ground beneath my feet.

Whoever she is, she'll be begging me to fuck her by the end of the day.

But when the door opens, my conviction turns to uncertainty as one of the only men that I truly respect appears in the doorway. Francis Valencia frowns at me, tilting his head to the side.

"Charlie?"

"Francis? What are you doing here?"

He frowns, grinning. "I, uh... I live here. What are *you*—I mean, pardon my manners. Please, come in," he stammers. "It's an honor. Tina!" He calls out over his shoulder. "Set another place at the table. The Prince is here."

"*What?*" Someone screams, and the crash of dishes shattering on a hard floor makes us both jump.

14

ELLE

THREE PLATES SHATTER at my feet. I don't even realize they've slipped out of my hands until there's broken ceramic spread halfway across the floor. Eyes wide, heart thumping, I glance at Tina.

"What did he just say?"

"The Prince, honey. It's okay, Frank knows him. Don't move, you'll cut your feet. I'll grab a broom."

"Dad *knows* him?"

What in holy Farcliff is going on?

Tina appears with a broom just as Frank and the *freaking Prince of Farcliff* walk into the kitchen. I'm frozen, trapped by the broken plates and unable to move a muscle as the Prince looks me up and down. His eyes are burning so hot I want to disappear, but I also never want him to stop looking at me like that.

"What happened?" My dad asks, glancing at the shards on the floor. "It's not like you to be clumsy."

"Don't worry, Francis, I often have that effect on people." The Prince smirks at me.

My face darkens as a blush stains my cheeks.

"Are all princes as presumptuous as you?"

I know I shouldn't speak to him like that, but he's here in *my* space. He's in *my* life. Prince Charlie isn't supposed to be here. He *can't* be here. I spent the last twelve hours convincing myself I'd never see him again.

"Elle!" Tina says, tutting as she sweeps the pieces of broken plate away from me. "Be respectful. This is our future King."

"Elle, is it?" Hearing my name on the Prince's lips does something to my insides, like a bolt of lightning straight to the pit of my stomach. "Nice to *formally* meet you."

Frank frowns, not understanding what the Prince means, and I have no desire to explain how *informal* our first meeting was. I clear my throat as Tina sweeps up the last bit of broken china at my feet.

"Excuse me," I mutter in a strangled voice, bolting to the bathroom down the hall.

The walls are closing in on me as I lock myself inside. I lean my back against the door, gulping down air as I squeeze my eyes shut.

He's *here*. In my parents' house.

My dad *knows* him?

I jump at a knock on the door. "Elle?" Frank's voice is full of concern. "Are you okay?"

"Yeah," I answer unconvincingly. "Be out in a sec."

His footsteps fade down the hallway and I take another breath. Glancing at myself in the mirror, I can't help but wish I'd worn makeup. I didn't exactly think I'd be seeing the Sex God Prince of Farcliff at my parent's Grimdale home, though.

I smooth my hair down and tug at my t-shirt. Why didn't I wear something more flattering? I'm not even wearing a proper bra. Squeezing my eyes shut, I shake the thoughts away.

What happened last night was just a one-time thing. The Prince doesn't care that I'm wearing an old t-shirt. He had his fun last night, and he's probably just here to see Frank.

Not me.

That's what I tell myself with every step that carries me back to the kitchen. It's an open-plan room, with a small dining table opening up into the living room beyond. My mom is putting out another set of plates as my dad and the Prince play with the dogs outside.

"Are you okay, honey?" Tina asks.

I force a smile. "Just a bit shocked."

"I was too, when Frank told me the Prince had been helping out at the shelter."

He what?

Tina shakes her head, smiling. "Prince Charlie has a certain... *reputation*, and I was shocked that he loves animals so much. He's really good with them." She nods to the backyard.

I stare at the two men outside, and damn it, she's right. One dog is rolling around at the Prince's feet, and another is sitting beside him, rubbing a big furry cheek on the Prince's royal freaking leg. Prince Charlie must feel my gaze, because he glances at me and a wicked smile tugs at his lips.

I look away. If Tina notices, she pretends not to.

So, we gather at the table and my nice, comfortable lunch with my adoptive parents turns into a decidedly *un*comfortable lunch with the man who screwed me senseless last night.

"How's training going, honey?" Tina smiles at me, as if this is a normal meal and there isn't literal royalty sitting to my left.

"It's good. Coach thinks I have a real shot at winning the singles event at the regatta this year."

"The Spring Regatta?" The Prince's eyebrows shoot up.

I force myself to hold his gaze, even though my entire body is burning up. I nod. "Yeah. On the Farcliff U team. I didn't qualify last season, but I've got a real chance this year."

The Prince frowns slightly, staring at my face more closely, and then nods. His knee brushes mine and a lump forms in my throat. I don't move my leg, and neither does he. The pressure of his knee against mine makes me want to faint.

I can hardly breathe. Charlie, on the other hand, eats as if nothing is happening.

He's toying with me.

"Of course you have a chance, Elle," Frank says. "You've done nothing but train since last year."

"It's still seven weeks away," I manage to say as the Prince nudges me with his leg again. "I've still got a lot of work to do."

I can't taste any of the food I'm putting in my mouth. I'm having trouble stringing simple sentences together, and breathing is becoming a serious problem. It feels like my whole head is bright red, even my scalp. All I can think of is the Prince's leg touching mine, and how much I never want him to stop.

This is very, very bad.

I turn to the Prince. "I hear you've been helping Frank at the shelter?"

I shouldn't have said anything to him, because now his gaze is on me. His eyes drop to my lips and heat zips through me, settling between my legs. I squeeze my thighs together and force another bite of food down.

"I have. Francis is one of the only people I've met that has truly good intentions. I try to do what I can to help." The

94

Prince tilts his head, looking at me curiously. "Do you always call your parents by their first names?"

I glance at Frank and Tina, smiling. "I'm adopted. But no, sometimes I call them Mom and Dad."

Tina's eyes sparkle. "I remember the first time you called me Mom. You were, oh..." she taps her chin with her finger. "You were seventeen years old, I think. I just about died of happiness. Three years it took for her to call us Mom and Dad."

I laugh, shaking my head. "Takes a lot for me to trust someone."

"I get that," the Prince says, his piercing gaze set on me. After a long moment, he glances at Frank again. "How are things at the shelter this week?"

"They're fine. Same as usual. What we really need is for people to spay and neuter their pets," Frank points his fork at the three of us in turn. "That would solve most of the issues we have with strays and abandoned animals. It should be a crime not to do it."

A small smile tugs at my lips as Frank launches into a speech I've heard a million times before. He's right, of course, people should spay and neuter—and he sees the worst of it every single day. All the abandoned, mistreated animals that have nowhere to go—Frank takes care of them. Every time he's forced to euthanize an animal, he comes home shattered, silent and heartbroken. When he finds a home for one of them—many times right here, until Tina puts her foot down as the house becomes overrun with animals—he's the happiest man in the Kingdom.

I steal a glance at the Prince. Apparently, he takes care of those animals too. In all the rumors I've heard about him, I've never heard anything about Prince Charlie liking dogs. It's always stories about women, and drinking, and fights. Or,

95

when he was younger, they were stories about illicit affairs with older women.

Nothing about volunteering at the Grimdale Animal Shelter.

"I've tried to petition the King to do something about it, Francis." The Prince shakes his head. "He won't listen. I promise as soon as I'm King, there'll be some new rules in place when it comes to pets. Your idea for a mobile spay and neuter unit is fantastic. I'd like to provide some funding."

Frank's eyes light up more than I've ever seen them. "Your Highness, that would be... well, that would be life-changing!"

Prince Charlie nods. "It's an easy solution to a big problem." He looks at Frank with a sparkle in his eye. "But I'll only do it on one condition."

"What's that?" Frank asks, his eyebrows tugging together. "Anything."

"Call me Charlie, for Farcliff's sake. How many times do I have to say it?"

Frank laughs, shrugging. "Old habits. If it makes you feel any better, I called our new dachshund Charlie." He motions over his shoulder to the little sausage dog jumping all over the older, bigger animals.

"You named your dog after me?" The Prince grins and I bite back a laugh. "That does make me feel better, actually."

"He may have named him Charlie officially, but Frank still calls the dog 'Your Highness'," Tina laughs. She looks at Frank with such love in her eyes that it makes my heart squeeze.

I stare at Prince Charlie as a laugh brightens his face, and it pulls at my heart. He actually cares about these animals, maybe even as much as Frank does. Sitting here, at our humble dining room table in the heart of Grimdale, it feels like he belongs.

In that moment, I realize I've judged the Prince a bit too harshly. There might be more to him than I'd previously thought.

As if he reads my thoughts, Prince Charlie flicks his gaze over to me and sends another wave of heat flooding through my body.

15

CHARLIE

I don't remember the last time I had a family meal. It was probably before my mother died, which means I would have been a small child.

I came to this house with the intention of finding out who Elle is... I'd never have imagined she would be Francis and Tina's daughter.

When the plates are cleared and lunch is finished, Elle gives Tina a hug. "Thanks for lunch, Tina. Delicious as usual."

"You're leaving already?"

"We have a team meeting. Coach gave us yesterday afternoon off for the..." Her eyes flick to me. "...for the people who were invited to the Prince's Ball, so we're meeting today to get focused again."

"Okay, well it was good to see you, Elle. Don't wait so long next time. You should come for lunch every Sunday like you used to."

Elle smiles, and I feel almost jealous.

I clear my throat as the two of them hug. "I should get

going as well," I stand up and shaking Francis' hand. "Thank you for having me."

"It was our pleasure," Tina wraps me in a big, motherly hug. It surprises me, but after a second I hug her back, squeezing my eyes shut. It's been a long, long time since someone hugged me like that.

I pull away and take a deep breath. Elle is already at the door, slipping on her shoes. She gives me a quick nod and waves to her parents before slipping out the door. I catch up with her at the Jeep.

"So, no goodbye for me? That's not very polite. Where's your respect for your Prince?"

"What are you doing here?" She asks, turning to face me. "Did you follow me?"

"Yes."

Her eyebrows jump up. She wasn't expecting me to tell the truth. "Oh."

"You never told me your name."

"Do you hunt down every girl you sleep with like this?"

"No, only you." I take a step closer as her breath hitches. The curtains in the house's front window move, and I grin. "They're watching us."

"They're watching *you*, Your Highness."

"Charlie."

"*Your Highness.*"

"You don't like doing what you're told, do you?"

"No more than you like minding your own business."

I grin. "You want to go for a ride?" I nod to my bike.

Elle's eyebrows draw together. She inhales, and finally shakes her head. "I actually do have a crew meeting. I wasn't lying about that."

"Afterward, then. I'll pick you up at Farcliff U."

An irresistible pink flush creeps up her cheeks as she

shakes her head. "No, that wouldn't... That's not a good idea."

"Why not?"

"Having the Prince of Farcliff show up to pick me up at a team meeting would be..." Elle bites her lip, searching for the right word. "A distraction."

"You didn't seem to mind the distraction last night."

"That was—"

"That was what?" My eyes narrow.

"Different." Elle turns her head away and I tilt her chin back to me with the tips of my fingers.

"I thought you were going to say it was a mistake."

"No," she whispers. "Never a mistake."

"So come ride with me tonight. I'll pick you up at home, so no one sees except Dahlia. She already knows what happened between us, doesn't she?"

Elle licks her lips, and it takes all my self-control not to kiss her right then and there on her parents' front lawn. She toys with the car keys between her hands, taking a deep breath. Finally, she lifts her eyes up to mine and nods. "Okay."

"It's a date."

"What should I wear?" She blushes right after the words blurt out and then shakes her head. "I mean... I don't know. Is that a weird question? Sorry. I don't really date."

"My preference is that you wear nothing, but that might not be convenient for riding a motorcycle," I say, leaning into her. Elle's eyes glimmer, and I continue. "Wear something you won't mind getting destroyed when I tear it off that perfect body of yours."

I hold her gaze for a few more seconds, as her eyes widen and her body tenses. I grin, taking her fingers in mine and kissing the back of her hand. "See you in a few hours, Elle."

. . .

WHEN I GET BACK to the castle, it feels like I'm floating. Not only did I find out who my mystery woman is, but she's *not* a Raventhal. Even better, she's the daughter of one of the men I respect most in the Kingdom. I don't care that's she's not a Lady or a Princess... in fact, that's exactly why I'm drawn to her.

She's different. Special. I can tell by the way she carries herself that she's been through a lot, and that makes me feel closer to her.

Before I make it to my wing of the castle, Talin materializes in front of me.

"The King would see you," he says, gesturing down the hall.

"The King can kiss my ass." I brush past him and Talin grabs my arm with a vice-like grip. I stare at his hand, trying to understand why or how this man is touching me without my permission. Dragging my eyes back up to his, I snarl until he lets go.

Talin takes a step back, clearing his throat. "His Majesty would like to discuss last night's events with you," Talin says a bit less forcefully, nodding his head down submissively.

"Well, tell His Gracious Ass that I'll be in my chambers. I can discuss whatever events he has in mind there." I stomp away from the man, my arm still burning where he grabbed me.

That man—that *snake*—is getting far too comfortable in this castle. He's weaseled his way to my father's side and won the King's ear, and I don't know what kind of lies he's whispering. I shake off the uncomfortable feeling that Talin always leaves me with and I make my way to my quarters.

It only takes my father a few minutes to knock on the door. He doesn't wait for me to answer before striding in. "You don't come when I ask you to anymore? Insolent brat."

"I stopped doing your bidding when you stopped treating me like a son."

The King rolls his eyes. "That was your own doing, boy. As soon as you fucked your own governess, I knew you'd never be fit to be King. But what can I do? You're my eldest son, and my hands are tied."

I ball my hands into fists, digging my nails into my palm to stop myself from screaming. The scandal with my governess was the last nail in the coffin of my tattered relationship with my father. He can't bear the fact that I'm his successor. I think it predates the shit with my governess. I think he's hated me ever since my mother died.

I take a deep breath and try to keep my voice steady. "What do you want?"

"I want you to tell me which Lady you've chosen as your wife."

"None of them." *The one I want isn't a Lady.*

"Excuse me?"

"You heard me."

My father's eyes narrow and he takes a step toward me. I fold my arms over my chest, cocking an eyebrow. I'm younger, stronger, and angrier than he is, and he knows it.

"Son—"

"Don't fucking call me *son* like the word actually means something to you."

He bristles, inhaling through his nose. "*Charles*, you need to declare a wife within three months. You're getting older, and it's time."

"Time for what? Time for me to follow all these stupid traditions?"

"You need a Queen."

"You're doing just fine without one."

"And who's fault is that?"

His words hit me like a sledgehammer to the gut. I wince, dropping my eyes and digging my nails further into my palms. "Fuck off. I just found her—that's all."

"Right after you dragged her up to that stupid cabin at Farcliff Lake. You know there are ticks and parasites in the forest."

"We never found out what killed her. How could a tick kill someone overnight?"

The King stares me down, and the familiar well of anger opens up inside me. I always knew he blamed me for my mother's death, but he's never come out and said it before.

I open my mouth, but nothing comes out. My chest feels heavy and grief tightens my throat.

My father grunts. "I've drawn up a list of suitable matches. You have two months to declare your betrothed."

"Father—"

"It's the *law*, Charlie. If you don't do this, you can't be King after me. As much as I would love for that to happen, I'm bound by the laws just as much as you are." He tosses a paper onto my desk. "Choose one of them, or I'll choose for you."

The door closes behind him with a bang, and my anger simmers under my skin. I stare after him, glued to the ground.

Finally, I stretch my hands out and shake out my shoulders. Walking to my desk, I glance at the thick paper with the royal letterhead that my father left behind. I skim the names of 'acceptable matches' as my lips curl in disgust. Crushing the paper into a tight ball, I throw it in the trash.

Fuck. That. Shit.

I've already chosen my Queen. She just doesn't know it yet.

16

ELLE

OLIVIA TITTERS after our meeting as the entire team crowds around her.

"It was right before midnight when he grabbed me. That's why the two of us disappeared from the ball. He took me up to his bedroom and ladies... the rumors are *true*." She holds her hands out in front of her, stretching them apart and wiggling her eyebrows. "He's big."

I know she's lying. The Prince was with *me* right before midnight—but still, her words irk me. Did he do anything with her before he found me? Or after?

Taking a deep breath, I try to ignore the little, insecure voice in my head that's trying to ruin this for me. I know Olivia is lying.

But what if it were true? The Prince doesn't owe me anything. He can sleep with anyone he wants. He probably does. I've heard the rumors. I've seen the tabloids. He's a womanizing jerk, and he never sees a woman more than once.

My chest squeezes at the thought, and I try to breathe through the tightness. I need to be logical about this.

How can that be true if he sought me out? He wants to see me again tonight, not Olivia Brundle.

The horrible little voices pipes up inside my head. I'm probably just the flavor of the week. I'm different from his usual flings, but he'll get bored with me, too.

I take a deep breath and push the thoughts away. Even though they're probably true, I'll just enjoy whatever is happening between us and keep the memory of it alive for as long as I live. The Prince isn't in love with me or anything, but that doesn't mean I can't enjoy the attention. I toss my bag over my shoulder and make to leave when Olivia stops me.

"How about you, Elle? How did you spend last night?"

"Not screwing the Prince, that's for sure," I say, staring at her.

Her face twists into a cruel smile. "That's obvious, sweetie. Even if you'd been invited, he wouldn't have looked at you twice. He prefers someone a bit more... womanly." She runs her hands down her sides and shrugs. "But I'm sure there will be some nice man who settles for you eventually. You just have to be patient."

I don't answer. I'm afraid if I say something, I might give in to the urge to rip her throat out with my bare hands. Instead, I turn around and walk out of the locker room as the rest of them laugh.

I seethe all the way back to my house until I can talk myself down. I don't know why I let those girls get under my skin so much. They mean nothing to me, so their words shouldn't hurt.

But they do.

Every time Olivia or Marielle or any of the rest of them say something cruel to me, it echoes in my head until I struggle to push it away. I'm confident in my studies and in rowing, but they know how to needle at all my insecurities.

They can sniff them out, buried deep in my heart. Those girls unearth my darkest fears and then hold them up and laugh at them.

Well, not tonight. I shove those insecurities away and get ready for my date. My date with *the Prince*. Olivia can say what she wants, it's *me* he's seeing tonight.

"What are you going to wear?" Dahlia opens the bathroom door and I peek around the shower curtain. She's eating a piece of toast and sitting on the closed toilet seat. She looks at me. "I think you should go for something sexy yet understated, so it looks like you're not trying too hard when in reality, you're trying really, really hard."

"Can we talk about this when I'm not naked?"

Dahlia frowns. "Why? Who cares?"

"Me," I laugh. "I care."

"You're so weird."

"Uh huh." I arch my eyebrows and she rolls her eyes, leaving the bathroom. She pokes her head through the open door again. "I'll pull some clothes from your closet and get them ready for you."

"Okay, thanks." I wait for her to close the door again. By the time I'm finished in the shower, Dahlia has half a dozen outfits for me to choose from. She talks me through all of them, why she chose them and why she thinks they would be a good choice.

I point to the jeans crumpled on the floor. "How about those?"

Dahlia just rolls her eyes and shoves one of the other outfits at me. "Wear that."

It's a tight black dress that I forgot I even owned and a pair of black tights. "I'm not sure this is motorcycle appropriate," I say. "I think the jeans are better."

"Jeans are not date-with-the-Prince appropriate."

"Maybe not, but they're very 'me' appropriate."

She stares at me sideways at me and I laugh. My nerves start to tense up and I take a deep breath. I glance at Dahlia. "Is this a bad idea?"

"What, the date? Why would it be a bad idea? He's the Prince!"

"I know, but... I mean, you know how I am. I can't really do one-night stands. I fall way too hard, way too fast—and always for guys that are bad for me. The Prince and me... that's literally a dead end. Never going to happen. No chance. So, what's the point?"

"The point is that you're glowing, and smiling, and I haven't seen you this excited about something besides rowing... probably ever."

"But..."

"You deserve to have fun, Elle. You deserve to feel pretty and to go out and have dates with attractive men who make you feel special. You deserve to have mind-blowing sex whenever you feel like it. I know that the rowing team is tough, and I see how mean those girls are to you. I think going out and doing something for yourself—just because you feel like it—is a good idea."

I take a deep breath and blow it out through my mouth. I nod. "Yeah, you're right. I just don't want to get all emotional over this and end up messing up my chances at the Spring Regatta."

"Well, make sure you use protection tonight and you'll minimize the chances of that happening."

I laugh, nodding. "Noted. Will do."

Eventually, Dahlia leaves my room and lets me get dressed in peace. I choose the jeans.

The Prince announces his arrival with a loud roar of his motorcycle engine as it tears down our quiet street. Dahlia squeals, jumping up and down as she fluffs my hair for the thousandth time. "You look amazing. Go get sexed up, you little hussy."

"I don't even know if we're going to have sex."

Dahlia just rolls her eyes as if I'm the dumbest person she's ever met.

I know what I *want* to happen—a repeat of last night. Perhaps multiple repeats of last night.

Whether or not that will actually happen, I can't be sure. I still don't understand what the Prince sees in me, or why he's shown any interest at all. I'm not royalty.

But my heart flutters and I grin at Dahlia. I'd say I have butterflies in my stomach, but they feel more like a flock of angry birds. They crash around inside me violently as I try to calm myself down.

The doorbell rings. I jump. Dahlia giggles.

When I answer the door, Prince Charlie stands there, wearing his motorcycle jacket and a bad-boy smirk. "Hey." He leans in, brushing his lips against my cheek.

I'm bright red already. "Hi."

He nods to his bike. "You ready?"

"I guess so."

"Don't sound too excited," he grins, extending his hand. I slip my fingers in his and an electric thrill runs up my arm. He leads me to the motorcycle, pulling out a spare helmet and sliding it onto my head. He looks deep into my eyes. "How does that feel?"

It should be illegal for a man to have such pretty eyes.

"Feels good," I say, knocking the helmet with my knuckles. "Solid."

The Pr—*Charlie*—laughs—as if everything I do surprises him. Maybe it does. He slips his own helmet on and swings his leg over the motorcycle. "Get on and hold my waist," he orders.

I do as he says, inhaling as I slip my arms around him.

"Hold on tight." I think I hear a grin in his voice. "Don't want you to fall off." My body is pressed against his, my legs hugging his thighs as the motorcycle purrs.

Then, we take off. I yelp, squeezing myself against him as we fly through the streets. My heart is in my throat for the first few minutes, but then I start to relax. Charlie has complete control over the bike, and I can feel him moving back and forth as if it's an extension of his body.

I lean closer to him, loving how our bodies fit together like this. He smells like leather with a hint of aftershave, and I inhale the scent deep into my lungs as the air whips around us. I close my eyes for a moment and a smile drifts over my lips.

This almost feels like rowing, except... *more*. It's the same feeling of slicing through the air, trusting the instrument underneath you as it carries you faster, faster, faster.

Charlie drives over to Farcliff Lake, taking a winding side road up to a private area of the park. We're entering the Royal Grounds. He slows the bike down as we climb up, up, up to the top of a hill, finally stopping at a lookout point on the southern tip of the lake.

I dismount, pulling my helmet off and trying to smooth my hair down. There's nothing glamorous about this, and I'm happy I opted for jeans.

Charlie glances at me. "What do you think? Enjoy the ride?"

"It's good. Reminds me of rowing."

"Yeah?"

"It's freeing." I smile. The Prince tilts his head, staring at me curiously. Finally, he nods.

I point to the lake below. "I've never been up here."

"You'd probably be arrested if you did."

"Right. My apologies, Your Royal Highness."

Charlie's eyes narrow and his jaw ticks. "You know what I want you to call me." He takes a step closer to me, taking the helmet out of my hands and placing it on the seat of his motorcycle.

I grin. "You know how I feel about following rules."

His eyes flash. The air between us gets heavy. I clear my throat. Being close to him makes me dizzy.

"Do you bring all your dates up here? A bit cliché, isn't it? Bad-boy Prince on his bike, taking chicks up to a romantic lookout?"

"Usually I just take them straight to my bed," he answers. "I don't waste time with things like this."

"Oh." I look away. Olivia's claim of sleeping with him suddenly doesn't seem so far-fetched. Maybe not at the Prince's Ball, but she might have done it another time.

He takes my hand, intertwining his fingers with mine and forcing me to look at him. "But with you, it doesn't feel like a waste of time. That's why I brought you here—cliché or not."

The flock of birds are back in my stomach, flapping so violently that I think the Prince might hear them. If he does, he never shows it. He just pulls me in and kisses me, and then leads me down a path I hadn't noticed.

It opens up onto a huge log cabin, nestled in the trees and hidden from the road. The cabin perches on the edge of a sheer cliff face overlooking the lake. The Prince leads me to the door, swinging it open and gesturing inside.

"Welcome to my home away from home."

17

CHARLIE

ELLE'S JAW drops when she walks inside. She cranes her neck to look up at the tall A-frame ceiling, and then swings her eyes around to the huge windows that dominate the far wall. With a small gasp, she walks up to them and looks out.

"This is gorgeous. You can almost see Grimdale from here! I didn't even know this place existed."

"My mother had it built when I was a kid. She used to bring me up here on the weekends whenever she could get away." My voice chokes up and I clear my throat.

Elle glances at me and reaches over to squeeze my arm. "I remember when she passed away." She smiles sadly. "I cried. I never knew my mother, and I always sort of hoped she would be like the Queen—really kind and loving." Elle glances at me and shakes her head. "Sorry. That's probably a stupid thing to say."

Usually, I hate it when people remind me of my mother's death. I hate talking about it and thinking about it. I hate the memorials and the pity in people's eyes when they think of my brothers and I left without a mother when we were just kids.

But Elle isn't looking at me like that. She looks genuine. I smile, letting my hand drift over her hip. "She was kind and loving. She'd have liked you."

Elle swallows as her cheeks flush.

I nod to the kitchen. "Drink?"

"Just water."

"Water?" I arch my eyebrows and Elle laughs.

"It's rowing season. No drinking, no parties, no drugs." She pauses. "No men."

"Well you're already breaking one of those rules. Why not a couple more?"

"The rules don't say anything about princes," she laughs. "I figured I could make an exception."

I pour us two glasses of water, and suddenly I'm nervous. Maybe I use alcohol as a crutch in these situations. Now it's just me, and Elle, and... that's it.

She takes the glass from my hands with a smile and keeps looking out the window.

"There's the Farcliff University Rowing Club," she says, pointing to the far end of the lake. "I can see the lights at the end of the pier. I usually row down to..." her eyes follow the shoreline, "...over here. To that buoy." A smile flashes on her face. "It's so different seeing it from up here. It all looks so small."

I stare at the buoy she pointed out. It's near the castle grounds, and I know the lake like the back of my hand. I turn to Elle. "Are you... Have you ever noticed a runner over there in the mornings?"

She turns her head slowly to look at me, her eyes widening. "Is that *you*?"

I laugh. "You're the rower?"

"I can't believe I've been racing the freaking Prince of

Farcliff every morning." A giggle escapes Elle's lips and she shakes her head. "Why do you do that? You can't outrun me when I'm on the water.'

I grin, shrugging. "I like the way you toy with me. You make me think I'm winning just long enough to dash my hopes when you finally pull away."

"Are you some sort of masochist?" She laughs and her blush deepens. "If I'd known it was you..."

"... then you wouldn't have acted like yourself, which would be a shame. I like you as you are."

Elle bites her lip, looking away and taking a sip of water. Her finger toys with the edge of the glass and smiles at me, shaking her head. "You're not how I thought you'd be."

"How did you think I'd be?" I ask.

"I've heard stories," she says slowly. "About you... with women."

"What kind of stories?"

Elle blushes again, and I fight the urge to crush my lips against hers. She shrugs, and I can feel the distance growing between us. "Stories of you... you know. You having sex and then demanding that the girls leave. A new girl every night. Models, actresses. That kind of thing. A player. Not really the type of guy that I would normally go for."

"Yet you're here."

"Yet, I'm here," she repeats with a tentative smile. "Despite all my better judgement."

I lead her to the couch and we put our glasses down on the side table. I drape my arm across the back of the sofa as she crosses one long leg over the other. She rests her head on my arm and looks at me.

"So, what kind of guy would you normally go for?" I ask with a grin.

That makes Elle laugh. "I don't know. I'm not exactly in high demand."

"You are to me."

She glances at me, frowning, as if she thinks I'm joking. I'm not. She's the most gorgeous, perfect creature I've ever laid eyes on. I run my fingers over her jaw and kiss her softly. Elle leans into me, curling her fingers into my shirt and pulling me closer. I inhale her scent, her skin, her flavor. I drink her in and kiss her more deeply.

She pulls away, leaning her forehead against mine. "Why did you bring me here?"

"What do you mean?"

Elle backs away a little more, staring into my eyes. She tilts her head to the side and shrugs. "I mean, you probably have women crawling all over you. What's your angle here? Why me?"

"My angle?" I scoff. "I can't just be into you?"

"You're the Prince of Farcliff, so no, you can't just 'be into me'. It doesn't make sense."

"I know who I am. Why wouldn't it make sense for me to be into you? You're the sexiest woman I've seen in my life. You're constantly surprising me. Is it so unbelievable that I would actually enjoy spending time with you?"

"Kind of, yes."

I pull away from her, frustrated.

She shakes her head. "Listen, I've seen pictures of your girlfriends. They look nothing like me. I don't know, Charlie —Your Highness—I just... I have a lot going on now. It might not seem like much, but rowing is really important to me. I need to perform well, and when I'm around you..." She sucks in a breath. "I don't know. You're super hot, and funny, and charismatic. You're literal *royalty*."

Elle takes a deep breath and stares at the ceiling. I don't really know how to react. This isn't how women usually act around me. Usually, a girl would be all over me by now—not trying to talk herself out of it.

She swings those big, brown eyes toward me. "This was a bad idea. I shouldn't have come. I might just be the flavor of the month for you, but that's not how I operate. I'm sorry to waste your time."

Elle shifts her weight to get up.

"Wait, stop," I shake my head.

"Thank you for everything. Last night was incredible, and this place is beautiful."

"So, stay."

"If I stay, I'll notice more things about you that I like, and it'll be that much harder when you get bored of me."

"Who says I'm getting bored of you?"

Elle laughs. "Every article I've ever read about you. Your reputation ever since you were, what? Fifteen?"

"That was different." Frustration bubbles up inside me. What happened when I was a teenager was different. Chaotic. *Wrong.*

We both stand. I want her to stay. I want to make her smile, and to know more about her. I want to *talk* to her and be around her—and then I want to fuck her brains out until the sun comes up.

"I'm from Grimdale, Your Highness. I don't even know who my parents were. I'm only at Farcliff University because I have a rowing scholarship. Getting involved with you..." She shakes her head.

"What?"

"It's a bad idea." Elle sighs sadly before leaning toward me and brushing her lips against my cheek. "Thank you for

117

bringing me up here. I don't think I'm the right girl for you, but I appreciate the time you've spent with me. You've made me feel beautiful and sexy, and I can't tell you how refreshing it's been. Thank you, from the bottom of my heart."

We stare at each other for a few seconds. She squeezes my hand and suddenly, panic starts to bubble up inside me. When she pulls away, I know she's going to leave.

I can't let her go. She's the first woman that I actually want to be around. She's the only person that I've actually wanted to talk to and cared about what she has to say. She makes me feel like she cares about me—not just my title. But Elle gathers her things and heads to the door as my heart starts to pound.

"Wait, Elle..."

She turns toward me, eyebrow arched.

"Don't go."

"I have to. I'm sorry, Your Highness, but I need to take care of myself. You don't understand the effect you have on me, and knowing that this... *thing* between us is going nowhere just makes it that much harder to be around you."

"It's not going nowhere."

"No?" Elle tilts her head, and I know she's right. She's from Grimdale, and I'm next in line for the throne.

I run my hands through my hair and take a deep breath. "I know I'm a dickhead to women, I know I have a bad reputation, but please stay. Please."

I've never begged a woman for anything. Elle toys with the zipper of her jacket. "I can't." She won't look at me.

"How are you going to get home?"

She shrugs. "I'll walk."

"Please, Elle. Don't write me off so quickly."

"I'm just trying to protect myself."

"So am I."

She frowns. I've never been honest about my past with anyone. I've never been this open with any woman—let alone a woman I only met the night before.

I take a deep breath. "Look, I know that I'm not exactly a poster boy for lasting relationships. I've been like this since..." I sigh, grimacing. "Well, things happened when I was younger. It... It's been hard to get past them."

Elle takes a step toward me, and the panic in my heart eases the slightest bit. "What do you mean?" Her head tilts to one side.

"Just... Give me a chance."

"For what, Charlie?" She smiles sadly. "What is this?" She points between the two of us. "It can never be more than what it is right now, and that's not enough for me. I may not have dozens of men lining up outside my door, but I need to have a bit of self-respect."

"You do. Elle, you're the most amazing woman I've ever met."

She laughs, shaking her head. "Laying it on a little thick, there, Prince."

"I mean it. I've never met anyone like you."

"Like what?"

"Someone who knows who they are and who treats me like a regular person. Someone who doesn't just fall over themselves to get with me. Someone smart and gorgeous and athletic, and..." I trail off.

Elle's eyes narrow as her lips curl upwards. "I never told you to stop."

I grin, taking a step toward her. "Stay for dinner. I made guacamole for the first time ever for you. I saw you eating it at the party—and I'm not too humble to say that for a first effort, it's damn good. Don't make me eat it by myself."

She bites her lip and her eyes flash. "Well... You didn't

mention there was guacamole involved. That changes things considerably."

18

ELLE

THERE'S a war going on inside me. My brain is telling me to leave, to protect myself, to walk away. My heart and my body are telling me to *stay, woman, are you insane?! Why would you ever leave?*

And, because I like living my life like it's a slow-motion car crash destined to annihilate me, I decide to stay.

I know it's a bad idea. This little relationship of ours is going nowhere. Even if the Prince says all the right things and makes me feel special, I know it's going to end.

But that doesn't mean it has to end *right now*, does it?

So, with a deep breath, I drop my purse and walk back toward the Prince. His face splits into a smile that melts my heart.

"Where's this guac?" I ask before he can speak. "Let's see what we're dealing with here."

Charlie laughs, scooping me up and spinning me in a circle. I love how easily he lifts me off the ground. The Prince nods to the kitchen. "This way, m'lady."

I follow him and sit on a stool by the kitchen island as the Prince takes out an assortment of foods from the fridge. He lays it all out before me—spreads, dips, cheese, charcuterie. The works. I'm impressed.

With a flourish, he pulls the guacamole out of the fridge and presents it to me. "Madame."

I take a chip between two fingers and dip it carefully into the guac. Our eyes meet and I grin.

When I taste it, I let out a deep, satisfied noise and nod in appreciation. "You did good, Charlie. This is decent guac. Did you really make it yourself?"

"Is that so surprising?"

"Yes," I laugh. "Absolutely. Did you do all this?"

He grins. "Not everything, no. I had some help. But I *did* make the guac."

"The guac is good."

Charlie settles down on a stool beside me and lays his hand on my thigh. It immediately sends a zing of heat coursing through my veins. We eat in silence for a few moments until I turn to him.

"So, why do you do the whole 'player' thing? Why go out with so many women so publicly, if that's not how you really see yourself?"

His face pinches. "I don't know."

"Not good enough," I say, dipping into the guacamole again. "If you can make good dip, you can answer a simple question."

"It's not simple. You're asking me why I am the way I am."

"I don't think being a womanizer is something to be proud of."

"I'm not proud of it."

"Could have fooled me."

He inhales sharply and runs his hand through his hair. He's done that a few times tonight, and I'm starting to like the way it makes him look. His face loses its sharp angles and for a moment—just an instant—I see another side of him. With his hair sticking up in all directions and his eyes focused inward, he looks like a different person.

Charlie sighs. "I've never told a soul about what I'm about to tell you, so, just... you know."

"I won't tell anyone."

He nods. "When I was fifteen, I fell in love with one of my teachers."

"The governess?"

The Prince winces. "Yeah," he sighs. "Miss Charlotte Thorne. She was..." He gulps. "She was beautiful, and graceful, and she was interested in *me*. For a fifteen year old kid..."

"... that's a big deal."

"We started hooking up." He swallows, playing with the edge of a napkin. "I thought I was in love." Charlie glances at me and shakes his head. "I found her one day poking holes through my condoms with a needle."

I gasp. "*What?* I never knew that. I just heard you had some illicit affair."

He scoffs. "They didn't print that in the tabloids, did they?"

I shake my head. "I just heard your father found out you were sleeping with her and threw her out."

The Prince snorts. "He found out because *I* threw her out. She went *mental*. Smashed every glass in my room, threatened me with a broken bottle. It was messy."

I sit there, not knowing what to say. "And you were fifteen? How old was she?"

He shrugs. "In her thirties, I think."

"Whoa."

The Prince sighs. "When my father found out what she was doing with the condoms, he got mad at me instead of her. Said I was irresponsible and not fit to be King. Told me I deserved to knock someone up and have to deal with the fallout."

I put my hand on his arm and he glances over at me, his eyes full of pain. My heart goes out to him. I know what it's like to have adults dismiss you. Lord knows I had to deal with my fair share of horrendous foster homes. But to hear that from your own father when all you need is support... That's rough.

"Charlie," I say softly. "You were a just kid. What she did was messed up. So wrong on so many levels. She was taking advantage of you."

"I wanted it," he says, shaking his head.

I take my hand and run it along his jaw until his eyes meet mine. I shake my head.

"You were a kid, Charlie. As much as you think you wanted it, it's not right. She should be in jail. I can't believe that wasn't reported publicly—all the news reports only talked about how you were a sexed-up teenager who couldn't control his hormones."

"I thought we were in love, and she was just using me to get a leg up in these fucked-up royal politics."

"She was taking advantage of you," I repeat, more slowly this time. "Do you understand? It wasn't your fault."

He shakes his head. "I knew what I was doing."

"You were a *child.*"

"I should have been more careful."

"It wasn't your fault." I squeeze his arm, forcing him to look at me. My words seem to sink in and he takes a deep breath. His eyes get watery and he clears his throat, looking away. There's so much about the Prince that I don't know—so much about him that I'll never know—but right now, I feel closer to him than I've ever felt to anyone before.

I run my hand over his back and lean my head on his shoulder.

"Do you really think that?" He asks softly. "That it wasn't my fault?"

I pull away, looking him in the eye. "Well, judging by what you've told me—yes, absolutely. I really think that. She was a grown woman, and she was using you in the most horrible way just to get ahead."

He nods, staring at the spread of food in front of us without moving. "I've never told anyone that before. Feels kind of good to get it off my chest."

"It's a lot to deal with." I nudge his shoulder with mine. "No wonder you're a womanizing scumbag, now."

His eyes flash for a moment, and then his lips curl up ever so slightly. He chuckles, and I throw another guacamole-smothered chip in my mouth.

"You'll pay for that comment," he growls.

"You make decent guacamole, though, I'll give you that."

In one smooth motion, he wraps his thick, strong arms around my waist and hauls me over his shoulder. I yelp, giggling as the Prince carries me down the hallway to the back of the lodge. His arm clamps down over my legs and I hang there.

Kicking the bedroom door open with a grunt, the Prince marches inside and tosses me down onto the bed. He rips his shirt off over his head and my breath catches. His eyes are dark, his lips twisted into a sinful smile. My blood pumps thick and hot in my veins as my body heats up at the sight of him.

Tattooed, muscular, and bad-boy perfect.

Crawling up on top of me, Charlie brushes his cheek against mine. The Prince's stubble scratches my skin as his breath tickles the base of my neck. He's taken me from zero to a hundred in an instant, and my body wants more. I want his touch, his tongue, his hands. I want it all.

Charlie sinks down on top of me, sliding his fingers up my sides and sending delicious shivers through my body.

Faster than I can react, he takes my hands and pins them above my head. Holding them up there, he kisses me fiercely.

In the depths of my mind, I know this is a bad idea. Sleeping with him once was bad enough—but twice? I can already feel myself falling for him. Pathetic, maybe, but I've always been this way. I can't help my feelings. I fall fast and I fall hard—and always at the worst possible time.

Even when I *know* it'll end in heartbreak.

Every second that I spend with the Prince makes me fly higher and higher, and I already know it'll make the crash back down to earth that much more painful.

But as Charlie lets out a soft growl and swipes his tongue into my mouth, claiming my lips and rolling his hips against mine, I'm not thinking about the inevitable fall. All I'm thinking of is his kiss, his body, his strength. I wrap my legs around his waist and let my desire take over, silencing my worries for now.

I can't help it. At this moment, Prince Charlie of Farcliff is on top of me. He's moaning into my mouth and holding me down like he owns me. He's cupping my breast and ripping my shirt in half. His hard cock is pressed up against me, and I can't think of anything else.

19

CHARLIE

I love the noises Elle is making. She moans and sighs, grunting as she bucks against me. It only takes a second to tear our clothes off each other. Elle is wearing lacy black underwear and a thin bra, and I smile. She knew I was going to see them tonight.

She shrugs off her now-tattered t-shirt and grins. "You're not very good for my wardrobe. Everything I wear around you gets destroyed."

"I'll buy you a new one." I crush my lips against hers as she wraps her arms around my neck. Elle's nails leave deep scratch marks across my upper back as she pulls me closer.

I've never brought a woman to this cabin before. This is my refuge, and I only ever come on my own—but having Elle here feels right.

Having her pinned underneath me feels *very* right. She wraps her legs around my waist and grinds herself against me.

My hands tangle into her short, brown hair as I bury my face into the crook of her neck. I inhale, drinking in her scent as my body goes into overdrive. I haven't felt this turned on in years.

Elle bucks underneath me and we roll across the bed so that she's on top of me. She grins, leaning her hands on my chest as I tuck my arms behind my head.

I grin. "You look good on top of me like that."

She grinds her hips slowly against me, curling her fingers into my chest. Her fingers trace my muscles—all the way from my pecs to my stomach, over every ridge and valley of my body.

"Do you shave your chest?" Elle runs the back of her hand back up over my chest. Her hips are still rolling against me in the most intoxicating way.

"I wax."

She grins, trailing her fingers over my skin.

"What?" I ask. "You don't like a waxed chest?" My hands are still interlaced behind my head and I glance down at myself, flexing. I buck my hips against her and she falls forward, giggling and catching herself against me.

Elle pokes my hard abdominal muscles and shrugs. "I like a little chest hair, to be honest. It's... manly. I don't know. It turns me on."

"I'll let it grow for you."

"You're planning on having me around long enough to see your chest hair grow?"

"I'm not the asshole you think I am."

"Jury's still out on that." Her eyes flash as a smile tugs at her lips. Hearing that from anyone else would piss me off, but Elle just makes me want her more. I like her sharp tongue. I'd like it even better wrapped around my girth.

She reaches down between us and feels my hardness before yanking down my underwear and pulling it off. This time, I have the presence of mind to use protection. I grab a condom from the side table and roll it on while Elle straddles me.

When she sinks down on top of me, I let out a soft moan. My hands grip her thighs as she rides me, splaying her fingers over my chest. Elle's eyes close and her mouth drops open.

We move together, grinding and thrusting and fucking each other wordlessly. She moans, dropping her chest to mine and holding me tightly.

Elle feels so fucking good, it makes my head spin. The way she moves her hips makes me want to explode right then and there, but I'm not ready to do that yet.

I flip her over again and she yelps, giggling. She twists her hands into the bedsheets as I give her a powerful thrust. Her mouth opens and she inhales sharply, squeezing her eyes shut and spreading herself wider for me.

Seeing her face like this—full of pleasure and lust and sin —is one of the hottest things I've ever seen. I drop my hand to her shoulder, dragging it across to her throat.

Elle looks at me through hooded eyelids, moving her hand on top of mine as I drive myself deeper inside her. She curls her fingers over mine, pushing my hand harder against her neck.

My cock is buried deep inside her and my hand is on her throat. My heart thumps as I squeeze a little bit harder. She exhales, closing her eyes and rolling her hips toward me.

I've been with kinky chicks before. Some of them were nuts. But this? Something about Elle just gently nudging me to choke her harder—that does something for me. The sweet, innocent girl that was ready to leave a few minutes ago is now completely under my control—and she fucking loves it. I drive myself deeper inside her as she wraps her legs around me.

I feel her come. Her walls grip me tightly as her back arches. Elle gasps, her lips dropping open as the orgasm rocks through her body. Her hands dig into my arms and I let go of her throat, pulling her up to my chest and holding her close as I come with her.

My orgasm hits me like a tidal wave as I empty myself inside her. We cling onto each other, trembling and panting until we finally collapse. As the pleasure subsides, I roll off her, staring up at the ceiling as my chest heaves.

"Holy shit."

She laughs weakly in response. "Yeah."

I turn to look at her, and she shimmies closer to me, her eyelids heavy and her body limp. I pull her into my arms and hold her, both our hearts thumping in unison.

We fall into a blissful kind of sleep for a few minutes, until Elle disentangles herself from me with a deep breath. "I should probably get going. I have practice at five o'clock tomorrow morning."

I groan. "That sounds horrendous."

"Maybe I'll see you there," she grins, "since you seem to enjoy losing our little races so much."

I laugh, pulling her into me and kissing her lips. She wraps her arms around me and I lay there, tangled in each other's embrace. Her skin feels like magic against mine. She smells incredible. I wish we could stay like this all night, but she pulls away from me.

"You don't mind driving me home?"

"Of course not," I answer.

Her smile is shy, but genuine. She kisses my shoulder and pushes herself off the bed to pull her clothes back on. I watch her get dressed until she leans over to grab my shirt, tossing it at my head.

"Perv."

"It's a nice view."

Elle laughs, shaking her head. I pull my shirt on as she holds up the ripped remains of her own top.

"Here," I say, pulling a drawer open. "Wear one of mine."

When she puts my shirt on, I grin. I like seeing her in my clothes. She brings the fabric to her face and inhales, smiling. "Smells like you."

I'm not used to this easiness. I feel more comfortable around her than any other woman I've ever been with. She doesn't treat me like I'm royalty, or a celebrity, or some kind of god. She's just herself. Without even trying, she makes me realize what I've been missing—the company of a woman that doesn't want anything from me.

She was ready to walk out on me earlier. She doesn't care that I'm Prince Charlie. She's not here because I'm royalty.

She's here because she wants to be. Because she likes *me*.

When we walk back to the kitchen, Elle stops to grab a bit more food. She munches on it, nodding and giving me a thumbs up.

"You did good, Charlie. Sex and snacks are on point."

I laugh, wrapping my arms around her. She hooks her arms behind my neck and smiles at me. I kiss the tip of her nose and inhale deeply.

"You okay?" Elle asks, tilting her head to the side.

"I want to see you again."

A flush stains her cheeks as a smile flashes across her lips. "You do?"

"Tomorrow."

She sucks a breath in and finally nods. "Okay. Tomorrow. Even though it goes against all my better judgement."

"Fuck your better judgement."

Elle laughs. "You have a special kind of way with words, Your Highness."

I tighten my hold on her and kiss her. Something shakes loose in my chest as I hold her close to me, kissing her more tenderly than I've kissed anyone before.

This girl is different. Special. The more time I spend with her, the less it matters where she's from. I'm starting to feel like I want to break all kinds of rules just to be with her.

20

ELLE

AND SO BEGINS the craziest time of my life.

If you'd have asked me a few weeks ago if I thought I'd ever see Prince Charlie in person, I'd have said *probably not*. If you'd have asked whether I thought he'd ever speak a word to me, I'd have scoffed.

If you'd have asked if I thought the Prince would ever rip my clothes off and fuck me like there was no tomorrow, I would have laughed and said *only in my dreams*.

Well, my dreams become a reality, and the Prince of Farcliff becomes my new lover. For the next three weeks, we spend almost every evening together at the lodge, and every morning he races me on the banks of Lake Farcliff. He makes me laugh and tells me I'm gorgeous.

And I feel beautiful.

Whenever Charlie looks at me with his dark eyes and even darker intentions, it sends a zip of heat rushing down my spine. When he kisses my forehead or strokes my arm, my heart thumps against my ribcage in the most intoxicating way.

I always had the feeling that guys settled for me when they couldn't get one of my hotter friends. Either that, or they liked my tits and didn't care about much else.

But not with Charlie. He makes me feel sexy and womanly and *wanted*.

Coach Bernard notices a change one morning as I put my shell in the water.

"You're awful smiley these days, Elle," Coach says, arching an eyebrow.

"Just looking forward to the Spring Regatta, Coach."

"I have high hopes. Keep training like this, and you'll have a chance at the title."

I row hard, I study, and I see Charlie. The Prince and I help Frank out at the shelter once a week, and Charlie has Sunday lunch with me at the Valencia's house. Dahlia grins at me non-stop.

I'm happy.

ONE EVENING, when Charlie is busy with a royal function, I lounge on the couch with Dahlia. A new season of *The Bache-lorette* is on, and Dahlia is explaining to me in great detail what she thinks of each suitor.

"I don't think I could handle having that many men trying to date me," I toss a piece of popcorn in my mouth. "It looks exhausting."

"I could do it," Dahlia responds, shrugging.

"Of course you could," I laugh.

She grins at me, and then winces as she grabs a handful of popcorn. "My period is so bad right now," she says. "All I want to do is sit here and eat."

I must make a face, because Dahlia sits up. "What?"

I shake my head. "Nothing."

Ever since I've lived with Dahlia, our cycles have synced up. Where mine was sporadic and irregular before, for the past year and a half I've lived with Dahlia, it's been like clockwork—just like hers.

Except... not this time.

"You okay?" Dahlia is frowning at me. "You look worried."

I shake my head. "It's nothing. When did your period start?"

"Day before yesterday."

"Huh."

"Why?"

"Nothing, it's just... It's nothing."

"Do you not have yours?"

I shake my head. "It's usually within a day of yours."

Dahlia brings her feet up onto the couch and rests her chin on her knees. "Maybe it's just late."

"Yeah. I've been training hard, could be that I'm just not eating enough."

"Yeah. Could be." Dahlia glances at me, swallowing. She bites her lip, and I know what she's thinking—what *I'm* thinking. What every girl thinks whenever her typically very regular period doesn't arrive exactly on schedule.

... *what if?*

"You never got the morning after pill, did you?" Dahlia asks, straight to the point as always.

I shake my head. "No."

"Have you guys been using protection? You and Prince Charming have been going at it like rabbits. I hope you've been responsible."

"I'm not pregnant."

"I know. I'm just saying..."

"I'm *not* pregnant."

"Maybe you should take a test."

"No." I shake my head. "I can't."

"Elle..."

"I'm not pregnant, Dahlia. I can't be. It was only one time! The chances of that happening..."

"... are not zero."

I take a deep breath and squeeze my eyes shut. No matter what Dahlia says, I just can't wrap my head around the idea that I could be pregnant.

No, not just pregnant. I could be pregnant with Prince Charlie's baby.

I sit up, putting a hand to my forehead and taking a deep breath. My mind immediately starts racing a million miles an hour.

If I'm pregnant, I'd have to stop rowing. I'd lose my scholarship. I'd have to stop college. How would I take care of it?

How would I tell the Prince?

The first evening we spent at the cabin, he told me about his governess taking advantage of him, and how much it had messed him up to find her poking holes in his condoms. I've seen him get rid of used condoms very carefully, and he's always extra safe.

I *know* he doesn't want kids—especially not with a nobody from Grimdale like me.

Putting a hand to my stomach, I take a deep breath and shake my head. "No. I'm not pregnant. There's no way."

"Just breathe," Dahlia says, scooting closer to me. She puts an arm around my shoulders and squeezes. "Your period will show up. There's been lots going on in your life, between your illicit love affair with the Kingdom's baddest bad boy, the biggest regatta of your rowing career, and your studies. Give yourself a break. Don't panic."

"I can't be pregnant, Dahlia. You don't understand."

"I do understand." She looks me in the eye, her face more

serious than I've ever seen it. "I understand perfectly, Elle. Don't panic. If it hasn't shown up in a few days, I'll buy you a test and we'll take it together. I'm here for you."

I nod. "Okay. You're right. It's probably just stress. Maybe I should eat more."

"Tell Coach Bernard to give you a day off, for Farcliff's sake," Dahlia says. "You need to rest. Between rowing and screwing the Prince, your body needs to recover."

"Yeah," I say, blowing the air out of my lungs. "I just need to rest."

"Give that coochie a break. Damn girl," Dahlia grins. "Tell Prince Charlie to take it easy on you."

"Shut up, Dahlia." I crack a smile and turn back to the television. "You're the one who had to buy a new bed frame last week. If anyone's coochie needs a break, it's yours."

"Hey, I take a few nights off a week," Dahlia says, tossing her rainbow-colored hair over her shoulder. "I know my limits."

"You don't know your bed's limits, though."

She just shrugs and grabs some more popcorn. "Let's order a pizza. Call it step one in Operation: Get Elle's Period Back."

"Deal," I grin, reaching for my phone.

I spend the evening with Dahlia, keeping my panic at bay. We watch a few shows, eat a bunch of food, and then we go to bed.

It's not until I'm under the blankets, staring at the ceiling, that I finally allow myself to think about it again.

What if I'm pregnant?

The thought of it terrifies me for a thousand different reasons. First of all, it would derail my entire life plan. My college degree hinges on my rowing performance, and I have a whole year left before I graduate. Falling pregnant now would mean losing my scholarship before I graduate.

If I don't graduate, I don't get a good job. If I don't get a good job, I can't provide for myself... or a kid.

I take a deep breath and put my hand to my stomach. I already know that if I were pregnant, I would keep it. Getting rid of a baby is out of the question. Giving it up for adoption isn't going to happen, either. I grew up in the foster system, feeling unwanted, tossed away like a piece of trash. I'm not going to do that to a baby.

If I were pregnant, I would be the best mother I could possibly be. If that meant dropping out of college and working for Frank at the shelter, or finding some other job, so be it. I'd make it work.

The thought gives me strength. It might derail my life plans, but what are life plans, anyway? Nothing ever goes according to plan. Meeting the Prince wasn't part of the plan. This whirlwind romance wasn't part of the plan.

I look down at my abdomen, wishing I had ultrasound-vision to be able to see what was going on in there. I take a deep breath to try to clear my head.

I'm panicking, and Dahlia's right. I've been putting my body under a lot of stress lately, and that's probably why my period is late.

What is it that Frank always says? *If you hear hoofbeats, think horses, not zebras.* There's probably a simple, common explanation. Not enough food. Too much training. Definitely not pregnancy.

I can't let my mind spiral out of control. What I need to focus on now is the Spring Regatta in four weeks. My performance at the regatta will determine my scholarship for next year, so that has to be my priority.

This romance with the Prince is fun, but it's a distraction.

Having an irrational pregnancy scare is just a sign that I'm not as focused as I should be.

I turn to my side and take a deep breath. I'll get some sleep, go to practice, and focus on rowing.

Easier said than done, though, when there's a big prince-shaped distraction in my life.

21

CHARLIE

I GET to the lakeshore at the usual time, waiting for Elle to pass by on her cool down lap. It's become our daily ritual, to run and row alongside each other. No one else knows that we do it, and it's one of the only times we can be in relative public together.

But this morning, she doesn't look for me. I see her row past without casting an eye toward the shore, and it stings. I stay on the edge of the water for a few more minutes, but she never reappears. I finish my run with a frown on my face.

Elle doesn't text me all day, which is also unusual. We've been in almost constant contact ever since that first night at the cabin. It makes me feel insecure and uneasy, and I don't like those feelings. They're not me.

By dinnertime, I'm angry.

My mind is spinning out of control. Who does she think she is, ignoring me? *Me*? I'm the fucking Crown Prince of Farcliff, and who is she? Fucking nobody.

At around seven o'clock, my phone dings with a new message.

Elle: Hey, I'm pretty tired and I have a big training session tomorrow. I might just take it easy tonight.

I read the text over and over again, trying to decipher exactly what she means. Am I being blown off right now? What's going on?

I pace up and down my room, staring at my phone every few minutes. I type out a response and delete it. Too angry. I type another one out and delete it again.

Third attempt.

Charlie: Sounds good. Get some rest.

I press send and sigh. None of my feelings are conveyed in that text. There's no way that Elle will know how off-balance I feel right now, or how badly I want to knock her door down and make her explain herself. Is she done with me? Is she tossing me aside like some used-up piece of garbage?

A rap on the door makes me jump. My brother Damon pokes his head in, along with our youngest brother, Gabriel.

"You all right?" Damon asks.

I run my fingers through my hair. "Yeah, why?"

"You look like you're about to punch a hole through the wall."

"I need to get out of here. Father's been asking me to choose a wife again, and I can't handle his bullshit right now."

Gabriel nods. "Better you than me. I'm glad I'm not the eldest. I saw him pull you aside last night. Who is he expecting you to marry?"

"I don't know," I sigh. "Some chick from Brundle. One of the daughters."

"Who, the blonde?" Damon barks out a laugh. "Is he trying to get you to end up with a messy divorce? She's already slept with half the Kingdom. Between your reputation and hers, no one would be safe."

"I think he's working on a trade agreement with Brundle," I say. "I keep hearing about this dam on the southern end of Farcliff Lake—the proposal that Mom was fighting fifteen years ago. He always shuts up about it whenever I'm around, though. I'm just a bargaining chip, apparently."

Damon grunts "That sucks. You can't even choose who you want to be with."

My thoughts turn to Elle. She knew this would happen. That's why she wanted to leave that first night. She knows that there's an expiry date to our relationship, but the more time I spend with her, the less I want that clock to run out. When I'm with her, I feel good. Normal.

Happy.

This is a time that I wish I could go and see Bo at the boxing gym. For weeks, I haven't needed the release of the punching bag, and it's because of Elle. She makes me calmer. But now, knowing that she doesn't want to see me, I can feel the aggression mounting inside me. I wish I could go down to the gym and hit the bags until I was a sweaty mess. Instead, all I can do is pace my room like a caged animal.

Damon tosses me my jacket. "Come on. We're going out."

"Where?"

"We were thinking Grimdale."

Taking a deep breath, I nod. I haven't been out in weeks, and it's not like I'll do anything else tonight. I may have been seeing Elle, but I'm not fucking married to the girl. I can still do whatever I want. And if she doesn't want to see me, then fuck it.

"Let's go."

Glancing at my phone once more, I see Elle's response.

Elle: Thanks xx see you tomorrow.

My heart squeezes. I don't want to see her tomorrow. I want to see her tonight.

But she's pushing me away, and I'll be damned if I'll ever grovel for a woman's affection. I did that when I was fifteen, and I learned my lesson the hard way. I throw my jacket on and follow my brothers through the castle hallways. We walk past the gym, and my thoughts snap to my first night with Elle.

That was the start of it all—the wild night that was never supposed to happen.

Well, whatever. I'm not going to let some chick hold me down.

I square my jaw and walk down to the garages. My brothers have already organized one of our drivers to take us to the Grimdale clubs. They're seedier than the Farcliff bars, but there's usually less press. Three princes can go and have a good time without being pestered with cameras and paparazzi.

When we get to the club, someone shoves a drink in my hand and I skull it in one shot. The alcohol sloshes in my stomach and I wait for the buzz to hit me.

My brothers were right—I need a night out. I need to loosen the fuck up.

I've been spending all my time either with Elle, or thinking about her. I haven't felt this way since I was a teenager, and that ended up being the biggest disaster of my life. If anyone were to find out that I was dating some orphan girl from Grimdale, all hell would break loose.

So, when my brothers find a gaggle of women, I let them put their arms around me. They nuzzle into my neck and I just sit there, drinking. I lap up the attention. I haven't had women fawn over me like this in weeks.

It feels good.

I'm the fucking Prince of Farcliff. This is how I deserve to be treated. But then, one of the girls whispers something dirty in my ear and I push her off me. It doesn't take long for security to drag her away.

Gabe frowns at me. "What was that about?"

"Nothing." I avoid his eye. I can feel his stare, and I know my brothers can tell something is wrong. A month ago, I'd have already taken at least one of these girls to a secluded part of the club and fucked her brains out. A month ago, I wouldn't have pushed that chick off me and had her kicked out of the club.

But a month ago, I hadn't met Elle.

I grab another drink and sit down. I can't stop thinking about her, and it's driving me crazy. I haven't seen her in twenty-four hours, and it feels like an eternity.

These feelings are too much. I won't admit to myself that I'm falling for her, so I just get wasted. Cameras flash, even here in Grimdale, and I ignore them.

None of this shit matters. Everything is a mess.

I'm falling for a girl that I can never have. She was right— we never should have gotten involved with each other. I should have let her leave the cabin that second evening we had together. I should have stuck to my rules, and not spent more than a single night with her.

But every time I look around the club, I see girls with too much makeup and not enough clothes looking at me with come-fuck-me eyes, and all I want to see is Elle.

No matter how much I drink, I can't get the image of her out of my head, and I can't ignore the feeling that she's pulling away from me, and I'm losing her.

So, I drink.

SOMEHOW, I wake up in my own bed.

Alone, thankfully.

That's not something that would normally be a relief, but today, it is. My head is pounding and my mouth tastes like ass.

I reach for my phone, but it's dead. Drunk Charlie doesn't charge his electronics, apparently. Groaning, I plug the phone in and stumble to the shower. I stand under the stream of water until I feel half-human again.

I forgot about this—about hangovers. For the past three weeks, I've been sober with Elle. I haven't woken up with a dead animal in my mouth and dull thumping in my head.

My phone lights up when I turn it on and notifications start pouring in. With every new ding, my heart sinks lower, and lower, and lower. The headlines are damning.

PARTY-PRINCE CHARLIE AT IT AGAIN
IS SHE THE ONE?
THREE PRINCES PARTY IN GRIMDALE

On, and on, and on.

Nowhere in my slew of notifications are any messages from Elle. I groan, flopping back down on my bed and covering my face with my hands.

My bedroom door opens. Neville walks in carrying a tray laden with a tall glass of water, two ibuprofen tablets, and a buttery piece of toast.

He knows the drill.

I grunt at him in thanks, and he bows. When he gets to the door, I stop him.

"Nev, how was I last night?"

"Sir?"

"I mean, how drunk? What did I do? Did I say anything?"

He bows again. "You were angry, sir. You said a name... Elle?" He stares at the carpet.

"What did I say about her?"

"You said... You said that you were fond of her."

"I said I'm fond of her," I repeat flatly, and Neville nods.

"More or less your words, Your Highness."

I grunt, and take the ibuprofen. I'm guessing my words were very, very far from 'I'm fond of her', but Neville is far too discreet to say it.

My butler just stares at me. "Will that be all, Your Highness?"

"Yes, thanks Nev."

When the door clicks shut again, I close my eyes and groan. I'm definitely *fond of her*. That's precisely the problem.

22

ELLE

I DON'T SEE the pictures until after practice, thankfully, but once I'm back in the locker room, I can't ignore the rest of the team crowding around their phones.

"He invited me out, but I wouldn't set foot in Grimdale." Olivia flicks her long, white-blonde hair over her shoulder and glances at me. "Not unless I wanted to get mugged."

"How original, Olivia." I roll my eyes. "I've never heard you make fun of Grimdale before."

"I'm just stating the facts."

"Facts? You've been mugged in Grimdale? How many times?"

She turns away from me with a huff. "Charlie just needed a break. He told me so last night, but I still wouldn't go there. I have standards. I mean, just *look* at the girls in those pictures. Can you say desperate?"

The girls all agree, and my blood turns to ice. Prince Charlie in Grimdale? With other girls?

I'm able to slip out of the locker room and find a quiet corner of the athletics building to look at my phone. No messages from Charlie, but a plethora of photos of him from last night.

My throat tightens and I squeeze my eyes shut.

I knew this would happen. I told myself it wasn't forever.

He and I are just a fling. It's not for real. It has an expiration date. It'll end.

Yet, I'm still not prepared.

Over the last three weeks, I've let myself believe the Prince Charlie cares about me, that he likes me, and that he wants to be with me.

Then, the first evening we spend apart, he's out partying —with other girls crawling all over him, kissing his ear. His *ear*! That's far too intimate for my liking.

Even though it hurts, I force myself to look at the photos and read the articles. Every image sticks another dagger in my heart. Every headline twists the handle and sends pain shattering through my chest.

He looks completely wasted in these pictures. Drunk, horny, and on the prowl in Grimdale.

And I thought he cared about me.

But who am I to be mad? It's not like we were exclusive, or anything. We never talked about 'us', or about what it meant to be together. I'm not his girlfriend. He's the Prince—do princes even have girlfriends?

Certainly not girlfriends from the poor end of the Kingdom that he keeps hidden away in a forest lodge. I should have been prepared for this. I should have been clear with him that I wasn't okay with this, and if that was a problem, I didn't want to see him.

I should have been stronger.

But he makes me weak, silly, and foolish. I practically asked for this to happen.

A tear rolls down my cheek. It's painful. Even though we

weren't explicit, spending every single evening with someone sends a certain message.

And that message is: I like you. I want to be with you. You matter to me.

To then go off and get drunk with a bunch of half-naked chicks hanging off each arm...

... that hurts.

A lot.

What can I do? I'm just Elle Valencia from Grimdale, and he's the Crown Prince of Farcliff. I pull myself up, wipe the tears off my cheeks and walk back home.

I beat myself up for feeling bad about this even though I knew it would happen all along. I feel like an idiot for thinking that I was special—that something significant was going on between us. That we had a future, or any hope of this ending without my heart being shattered.

By the time I make it home, I'm ready to get in the shower and have a good cry in private. I feel like a fool, and I just need to get all this emotion out in order to figure out how I'll break things off with Charlie.

I don't get to do that, though, because sitting on my front stoop, holding a bouquet of white roses, is none other than the Prince himself.

Charlie stands as I walk up the path. His face is lined and he looks hungover as hell. "Elle..."

"Hey."

"These are for you." He thrusts the roses toward me.

I take them and nod. "Thanks. Why?"

"Why what?"

"Why are you giving me flowers?"

The Prince runs a hand through his hair and sighs. "I went out last night."

"I heard."

He stares at me for a moment and sighs. "I didn't do anything."

"What's that supposed to mean?"

"I mean I didn't sleep with any of those girls in the pictures."

"Okay. Um, congratulations? Do you want a gold star?"

He sucks in a breath. "You're mad."

"I don't know how I feel. What are we doing, Charlie? This isn't going to end well. I know it, and you know it..."

"So, what? You don't want to see me?" His eyebrows draw together and he gives me the biggest, princeliest, most puppy-dog eyes I've ever seen, and I know I'm too weak to turn him away.

My shoulders drop. "Let's go inside. I need a shower."

Charlie follows me in, and I put the flowers down on the desk in my room. I drop my gym bag and sit on the edge of my bed. The Prince closes my bedroom door and watches me for a moment. "Are you mad at me?"

"I'm mad at myself, mostly," I answer with a dry laugh. "Listen..." I sigh.

I want to tell him to go, to leave me alone, to not string me along like some pathetic groupie until he gets sick of me...

... but the words won't come out.

Charlie walks toward me and slips his hands into mine. He pulls me up off the bed so I'm standing in front of him, my chest pressed against his. He takes my hands and hooks them around his neck before clasping his own behind my back. Resting his forehead against mine, he takes a deep breath.

"I was upset you didn't want to see me yesterday, so I got drunk. I didn't touch any of those girls. I had the one in the white dress kicked out of the club. I swear, Elle, I was thinking of you all night."

My heart thumps and my emotions war inside me. "There's no future between us, Charlie. You know that, right?"

"Why not?"

I laugh, pulling my head away from his to look at his face. "What do you mean, why not? Because I'm me, and you're you. We've been sneaking around for almost a month now, but then what? You're going to go public with your Grimdale girlfriend? It's never going to happen."

"I'll go public right now, Elle. Here." He takes out his phone to take a picture of us and I push his arm away, laughing.

"Come on." I shake my head.

"I'm serious."

We stare at each other, and I finally sigh. "I didn't like seeing those pictures. I get that you like to go out, but..."

"I was thinking of you, Elle. I was always thinking of you."

"But you still let them crawl all over you."

"I know. I fucked up, and I'm sorry. I want *you*."

I want to believe him. My heart believes him, but I know I'm setting myself up for a long, hard fall. There's no future between us—that much is certain.

But hope is a wriggling little worm, a termite that makes its way to the depths of my heart and burrows itself inside me. It's a low flame that burns deep in my soul and softly whispers *what if...*

Hope is a dirty liar, but I still choose to believe it.

I choose to believe the Prince when he says he was thinking about me and when he says he didn't do anything with any other girls. I believe him when he says we might have a future together, even though I know it's not true.

He tilts my chin up toward him and kisses me tenderly, and then he strips off my clothes. I undress him, laying a soft kiss on his chest, brushing the outline of one of his tattoos. I sigh, giving in.

I want him.

I'm not ready to let him go.

The two of us head to the shower together. Under the stream, we wash each other and the Prince makes me come with his hands, his mouth, his cock.

"Come away with me this weekend," he says, holding me tight as I try to regain control over my shaking, post-orgasmic legs.

"What? Where?"

"To our country house. Let me treat you like a princess."

I brush his wet hair off his forehead and place a kiss on his lips. "I can't, Charlie. I have practice. I can't miss any training sessions this close to the regatta."

He pouts, which makes me chuckle.

"After the regatta, we'll go away together," he commands.

I smile. "Okay. After the regatta."

But I'm not sure there will be an 'after the regatta' for us. This feels like the beginning of the end, only neither of us are admitting it.

23

CHARLIE

I LEARN a few things that day.

Number one, I learn that I really, *really* care about Elle. I care about her enough to grovel.

Number two, I learn that partying and girls don't have the same draw as they once did.

And number three—perhaps most surprising—is that I learn my father is having me followed.

When I get home from Elle's house, Talin appears out of thin air and points down the hall to my father's study. When I step inside, my father is fuming.

"Dahlia Raventhal? Really? One Raventhal bitch wasn't enough? We invited the girl to the Prince's Ball, but I wasn't expecting you to fuck her."

"Excuse me?"

"I know you've been sneaking around with someone, but I didn't expect it to be Raventhal filth," he spits.

"You think I'm sleeping with Dahlia Raventhal?"

"Don't play innocent with me, Charles. How many times do I have to tell you that you need a *suitable* wife?"

"Suitable for who, Father?"

"For the Kingdom!" His voice booms as it echoes around his office. He huffs, his neck wobbling as he glares at me.

I flop down onto one of his chairs and stare at my nails. I can feel my father's anger ratchet up a couple notches, and my lips twitch.

"You are the Crown Prince of—"

"I know who I am, and I also know that it's the twenty-first century. You don't need to marry me off to some princess for political reasons. We have actual politicians for that, now."

The King's face turns bright red. He pinches the bridge of his nose. "Don't be naive, Charlie."

"Naive? You think I'm being naive?"

"You were naive when you almost impregnated your governess, and now you're going to bring dishonor on our family by doing it again."

The air between us grows tense.

My eyes narrow. "Why are you so worried about my marriage all of a sudden?" I glance at his desk and catch a glimpse of some contract documents. My blood boils. "The Farcliff Dam Project? That was thrown out fifteen years ago. Mother saw to that. We would need to relocate the entire population of Grimdale."

"Things change in fifteen years, Charles." He waves a hand. "And I'm worried about your marriage because it's time. The law states that you need a wife to become King, and I'm sick of you being such a fuck-up. Dahlia Raventhal is just another one of those fuck-ups of yours."

The King shuffles the papers away, shoving them into a drawer in his desk. My father is planning something, but I don't know what. Something about him pushing this marriage all of a sudden—it makes the hairs on the back of my neck prickle.

Something doesn't add up, and my father is a dangerous man.

Dahlia Raventhal is from a suitable family—but I'm not sleeping with her. She's not the reason I went to that house today.

No, the truth is much, much more damning.

At least Dahlia Raventhal is from an old family. My father wouldn't dare do anything to hurt her. Elle, on the other hand...

Elle doesn't even know who her parents are. If my father is following me, he's up to something, and I don't trust him to be an honorable person. The last thing I want to do is put Elle in danger. The King could hurt her without any repercussions. If he knows that I care about her, he could throw her in jail or pull her scholarship—or worse.

He could make her disappear without a trace.

I swallow and square my shoulders. If my father thinks I'm interested in Dahlia Raventhal, then at least Elle is safe from his wrath.

"What are you going to do about Dahlia?" I ask. "Since you seem so sure that I'm seeing her."

A smile twists his lips. "I'm going to invite the Miss Raventhal to the castle, and you're going to declare your intentions with that Raventhal swine." My father sits down again and waves a hand. "You can go."

Talin opens the door and I storm out within another word.

I walk straight to Damon's chambers and push the door open. He looks up from the stack of notes and books on his desk, tucking a pencil behind his ear.

"Charlie, what's up?"

I look at my brother and take a deep breath. "I need your help."

. . .

DAMON and I park the car in front of Elle's house, and my brother looks over at me.

"You sure about this?"

"No, but it's the only solution I can think of."

"You owe me one." Damon grins

"I know."

We exit the car and walk up to the house. The lawn needs to be mowed, and the paint is peeling. I wish I could use the resources of the Crown out here to get Elle living in a half-decent place, but I can't. Now that I know my father is watching me, no one can know about her.

When Elle opens the door to see me, her eyebrows shoot up. "Hey. What are you doing here? Is that...?"

"Elle, this is my brother, Damon."

"Miss Valencia," Damon says with a deep bow. Elle looks at me, surprised.

"Uh, hi. Come in." She opens the door wider for us and we step into the narrow entryway.

"Who's there?" A voice sounds from down the hallway. Dahlia Raventhal's multicolored head appears from around the corner, followed by the rest of her completely naked body. She glances at the three of us and waves a hand. I look away, but not before I learn that Dahlia Raventhal dyes her pubes to match the hair on her head.

Lovely.

My brother doesn't look away so quickly. His eyes bug out of his head and he stares at her until she disappears into a side room.

Elle sighs. "That's my roommate, Dahlia," she says, glancing at Dahlia's doorway with a sidelong glance. "She doesn't really believe in clothing, in the traditional sense."

"That's totally fine," Damon says, still staring at the room where Dahlia disappeared.

Elle leads us down the hallway toward the kitchen. I slide my hand down her lower back and she nudges into me. "What's going on?"

"I need to talk to you... and Dahlia."

She frowns, but gestures to the kitchen table before going back to knock on Dahlia's door. When the two of them reappear, Dahlia thankfully has a robe on. I'm not sure Damon would be able to focus long enough if she were still naked.

The girls offer us water and coffee, but I shake my head. Elle takes a seat next to me and slides her hand over my thigh, her eyes questioning. Dahlia hums to herself as she rummages through the refrigerator. My brother's eyes are glued to her robe-covered ass.

I take a deep breath. "Dahlia, I have a favor to ask."

"What is it?" She asks without looking back. She pulls out a leftover rotisserie chicken from the fridge, ripping off a chicken leg before taking a bite. Munching on it, she turns to the rest of us and arches her eyebrows.

Elle stifles a smile and I exchange a glance at my brother. Dahlia holds out the plate of chicken. "You guys want some?"

"Uh, no. Thanks." I clear my throat. "Listen, Dahlia, I was wondering if you'd mind pretending to be in love with my brother."

"What?" Elle turns to me, frowning.

Dahlia shrugs. "Sure." She tosses a chicken bone into the garbage and licks her fingers. Damon licks his lips.

"Wait, no, Dahl. Don't just agree to this. What are you talking about, Charlie?"

"*Charlie?*" Damon's eyes finally leave Dahlia and come to rest on Elle. He knows that no one calls me Charlie unless they're very, very close to me.

I take a deep breath. "My father saw me come here. He thinks I'm here because of Dahlia, which would understandably cause some controversy. He's going to invite you to our place for dinner, Dahlia, so I was thinking if I say that I was here to come get you for Damon..."

"... your place as in, the castle?" Dahlia asks, her eyebrows drawing together. "I don't know. I'm not..."

"Yeah. Is that a problem?"

"Can we just back up for a second?" Elle stands up, putting a hand to her forehead. "What the hell is going on?"

"Look, it's no big deal," Damon interjects. "My brother likes you, but he's the Crown Prince, so it's complicated. He needs a bit of time to figure out how to make that work. If my father thinks he's into Dahlia, it means you're safe. If my father thinks he's into nobody, even better. I'm going to buy him some time by saying that *I'm* the one who's into Dahlia," he swings his eyes to the short fairy-like girl who's still munching on rotisserie chicken, "and then you'll be free to keep seeing each other without fear of retribution. Simple."

Damon smiles at Dahlia, who nods and smiles back.

Dahlia looks at Elle. "Seems simple to me."

"What do you mean, if he doesn't know about me it means I'm 'safe'?" Elle says, looking from me to my brother. "Am I in some kind of danger?" She stands and starts pacing the room. I can see the panic mounting inside her.

"No," I answer, standing up to stop her pacing and put my arms around her. "No. You're not in any danger. I'll protect you."

"From what?"

"Look, Elle, I just need time to figure this out. I want..." I take a deep breath. "I want you. For real, I mean—in public, for everyone to know. I don't want to sneak around anymore, but there are traditions that go back centuries, and ignoring them will cause... ripples."

"Ripples?" Elle's eyes widen. She bites her lip and looks at her friend. "And you're okay with this, Dahlia? What about going to the castle?"

"Is that a problem?" I ask, pulling away from Elle. I wasn't expecting this kind of pushback when I thought of this plan. I thought Dahlia Raventhal would be more than willing to play along.

Dahlia shifts her weight from foot to foot and puts the plate of chicken down. "It's not a problem, per se. I just... I'm not really a castle person." She smiles awkwardly. "You know?"

"Definitely," Damon says, running his hand through his hair. "I know what you mean."

Dahlia's eyes brighten. "You do?"

"You do?" I say, arching an eyebrow.

Dahlia chews her lip and looks at Elle. "I'll go, if it means it'll help Elle."

I exhale in relief and Damon smiles. Elle frowns, but finally nods at her friend. "Okay, but only if you're sure, Dahlia."

"I'm sure," Dahlia says. She turns to Damon and smiles. "Maybe we should come up with some kind of back story."

"Yeah, definitely. What are you thinking?" Damon's face brightens as Dahlia sits beside him.

Elle still looks unsure, so I lead her into her bedroom and wrap my arms around her. I kiss her forehead and hold her tight. "I'll figure this out, Elle."

She forces a smile and nods. "Okay. Just don't hurt Dahlia for my sake."

We stay there, arms around each other, and I'm not sure how to respond. The more time I spend with Elle, the more strongly I feel about her. But things aren't as simple for me as they are for commoners.

I do know one thing, though. I want to be with Elle, and no one—not even my father—will stop me. Traditions be damned—I've chosen my woman.

24

ELLE

WHEN PRINCE DAMON and Charlie leave, Dahlia doesn't seem bothered at all. Me, on the other hand? I'm very disturbed. I knock on Dahlia's bedroom door frame and poke my head through the opening.

"What do you think they meant by 'keeping me safe'? Do you think I'm in danger by sneaking around with the Prince like this?"

Dahlia is in bed reading a novel. She puts the book down on her side table and pats her bed for me to come and sit down next to her.

She takes a deep breath. "I don't really know. If Charlie wasn't the eldest, it would probably be easier. He's the heir to the throne, so who he dates is a big deal."

"No one seemed to care before."

"He wasn't twenty-five before. You know the traditions. He was also never with the same girl for more than a night or two until he met you." She smooths her hands over her robe and takes a deep breath. "I think he likes you."

"I should never have gotten involved with him."

"Don't say that," she says, smiling at me. "You've been

happier than I've ever seen you. And you said yourself, your training is going well, even though you're always tired from your marathon sex sessions. I think having regular sex has helped you relax."

I can't help but chuckle. "Does everything always revolve around sex?"

"Sooner or later, yeah," Dahlia shrugs, "but I think Prince Charlie likes you a lot."

"It's kind of irrelevant, though, isn't it? Even if he does like me, this is what has to happen. He has to pretend he doesn't even know I exist." I shake my head and sigh. As much as Charlie makes me feel amazing—sexy, smart, womanly, you name it—I just can't shake the feeling that this relationship is doomed.

If he can't tell anyone about me... what's the point?

I should have more self-respect. A little voice in my head gets louder, screaming that *this is the same thing that always happens with men.* Charlie doesn't actually like me enough to go public with me, and there's no future for us. I'm just a fun distraction, and when he gets bored with me, it'll be over.

If he can't introduce me to his family, where is this relationship going?

Nowhere, that's where it's going.

Dahlia nudges me. "Hey," she says. "Get out of your head. It'll be fine."

"You don't know that."

"No, but I know the regatta is in a month, and you need to focus on your training. I'll go to this dinner, and the Prince will come here and tell you how much he loves you, and everything will work out."

I scoff. "He doesn't love me."

Dahlia just rolls her eyes. "Uh huh."

"You're right, though. I need to focus on training. I had a

bad session on the water this morning. I think I was stressed. I'm not used to feeling like this... all out of control and off-balance."

"I know," Dahlia says with a smile, "but you also haven't been sleeping as well. You should go to bed earlier, you'll feel better. This whole insomnia thing is no bueno. Just focus for one last month before the end of the season. We can deal with the Prince afterward." She wraps me in a hug.

"You don't mind going to the castle?"

Dahlia sighs, looking away from me. "It'll be fine."

"What happened with you and your family, if you don't mind me asking?" I look at my roommate and I realize that I don't really know that much about her. "Why are you so apprehensive about the royal family?"

I only learned a few weeks ago that she comes from an aristocratic family, and now I'm realizing that there's more to her story. Her mother used to be the Queen's best friend, but there was some controversy when she died. Raventhal became a bad name in Farcliff.

I only learned who Dahlia really is because of the Prince's Ball, and I never would have known her last name was Raventhal if I hadn't seen that invitation. I'm starting to think there's a lot about her past that I don't know—I just know she doesn't want to be part of the royal world anymore.

The fact that she's willing to go to the castle to cover for me is a testament to what a great friend she is.

Dahlia smiles sadly. "I'll tell you some other time. I just don't like castles and traditions and rules. They don't really work for me."

I grin. "Yeah, I can see that. Well, thank you. I appreciate it."

She sighs, putting a hand to her chest. "I'll do anything for young love."

"You keep saying that word," I laugh. "I don't think..."

"... oh, shush," she interrupts with a laugh. "Love is love whether you want to admit it or not."

OVER THE NEXT FEW DAYS, I follow Dahlia's advice. I focus on training, and put in some decent sessions on the water. I go to bed earlier and try to shake this persistent tiredness that seems to have settled deep in my bones. Prince Charlie and I still see each other every day, but I can feel my heart starting to close itself off to him. I know that this is going nowhere, and I'm preparing myself for the inevitable—for the day he'll tell me it's over.

Self-sabotage, anyone? Yeah, it's my specialty.

The regatta is only three weeks away, and I need to be focused on rowing, not on my doomed love life.

Dahlia receives the invitation to the royal dinner on a Wednesday evening on the same thick, watermarked paper as the Prince's Ball invitation. The envelope smells like perfume, and a little tendril of jealousy curls inside me.

It's just yet another reminder of the world I'll never belong to.

My life is just one big rejection, from the time I was born and put into foster care, to being the Grimdale outcast at college, to not being able to be out in public with the first guy who seems to really care about me.

But I just tuck the jealousy away and watch Dahlia get ready to go to the castle. She looks gorgeous, and when the limousine comes to pick her up, she steps into it as if she's always been picked up outside her house by limos.

She looks like that because she *has* always been picked up by limos. She's Dahlia Raventhal.

And I'm nobody.

I sigh, pushing the thoughts down. My phone dings.

Charlie: Wish you were here.

I smile, and my heart eases. At least he's thinking about me.

DAHLIA DOESN'T GET HOME until almost midnight. I hear her go straight to her bedroom and close the door, and I know I'll have to wait until tomorrow to hear about the dinner.

Still, sleep evades me, and I know my training session in the morning will be painful.

AS IT TURNS OUT, practice is, in fact, painful. Coach Bernard notices, and he pulls me aside after training.

"What's going on with you, Elle? Your last few sessions have been piss-poor."

"I know, Coach. I haven't been sleeping well."

He harrumphs, pursing his lips. "This is a crucial time, Elle. I need you at your best."

I sigh, dejected. I can't meet his eye. He's right. I should be pushing myself harder with every practice for the next week, and then ease off the week before the regatta. As it is, though, my peak weeks of training are not going well. My stomach gurgles and I feel sick as Coach Bernard studies my face.

I feel like I'm going to throw up.

Coach Bernard puts a hand on my shoulder. "Take tomorrow and the rest of the weekend off, Elle. Come back fresh on Monday."

"Really?"

"Maybe I've been pushing you too hard. You look like you need some sleep. At this point, it's better for you to be rested than it is to kill you with extra training sessions."

His eyes soften and he squeezes my shoulder. Gratitude floods my chest and I breathe a sigh of relief. "Thanks, Coach."

It's Thursday, which means I get three whole days off. Three days! I haven't had three days off in months. I go home and collapse onto the couch, exhausted. Dahlia walks into the living room soon afterwards, clutching a hot water bottle to her stomach.

"Have I mentioned how much I hate my period?" She flops down beside me with a groan.

I stiffen.

She notices.

"Dahlia," I say, my voice barely above a whisper. Terror ices my veins. "I think it might be time to take that pregnancy test."

25

_____

CHARLIE

THE DINNER PARTY GOES WELL, all things considered. Damon and Dahlia do a remarkably good job of pretending to be into each other.

My father throws me a couple suspicious looks throughout the meal, but he seems to take the bait. He's not overly pleased that Damon is supposedly interested in a Raventhal, but at least he isn't the heir to the throne. He doesn't need to choose the perfect wife for himself and the Kingdom.

No, that responsibility falls squarely on my shoulders.

After dinner, I follow my father out of the dining room.

"Happy?"

He arches a wiry eyebrow at me and grunts. "No, but at least she won't be Queen."

"She seems all right to me."

"Have you forgotten our history with the Raventhals?" He spits the words at me, as if the accusations about my mother's death were my fault. "Tabitha Raventhal brought shame on this family, and now I'm supposed to entertain her daughter as if nothing happened."

Anger flares through me, and I take a deep breath to push it down. Now is not the time. We just had an almost civil dinner together, and I don't want to sour it ten minutes after it's over.

"Father, things have changed. Who cares about that? It's in the past."

"Well, it may be in the past but I'm still glad she's not going to be your wife."

"Who cares who I marry? Why does this matter so much to you?"

"I care," he says, squaring his shoulder as he turns toward me. "Who you marry will claim the throne with you and will carry the heir to the throne of Farcliff. How do you not realize the importance of that?"

"Yeah, but it's a largely meaningless title," I scoff. "We have a cabinet, and ministers, and an entire government. You don't need me as some chattel to sell off to whichever Lord wants to do a deal. Is this why you've been pushing me toward Olivia Brundle? For that stupid dam project?"

"You're too naive, son."

"I'm not naïve. I'm living in the twenty-first century. Unlike you."

"When will you understand the responsibility on your shoulders? I blame your mother for this. She spoiled you with ideas of independence. She didn't understand the magnitude of her position, either."

"Don't speak about my mother like that." My voice darkens and I take a step closer to him.

My father snarls. "She was a fool, and she died because of it."

"Don't you fucking say another word." I take another step and my hands ball into fists. My father stares me down as the air between us thickens. A bead of sweat trickles between my shoulder blades as my heart pumps hot, angry blood through my constricting veins.

My mother's death was the most devastating moment of my childhood, and I always thought the King blamed me for it—but now, when he looks at me like this, I'm not so sure. He seems almost glad she's gone.

"It's just a shame that she didn't take you with her," my father says in a low voice. "Damon would make a much better King."

His words sting, hitting me like a slap in the face. I watch him walk down the hallway and I stay rooted in place.

WHEN I SEE Elle the following day, she seems distant. We drive to the cabin—our second home together—and she stands near the windows staring out.

I point to the outlet of the lake on the near shoreline. "There's a proposal to build a hydroelectric dam right there. It would provide power for all of Farcliff, but we would need to relocate everyone in Grimdale."

"What? That's crazy! Are they allowed to do that?"

"Not technically, no. My mother fought the project when she was alive and it was denied by the planning commission. That was fifteen years ago, though, and I've seen paperwork for it in the King's office."

"She always did seem to care about Grimdale more than most royals."

I smile, remembering how my mother would take me down to see Bo at the boxing gym, or to volunteer at different charities. "She was special."

"What's going to happen with the dam?"

"I'm not sure. My father won't be able to push it through without government approval. I haven't seen anything official about it. I don't know if him pushing my marriage is related at all. I just... I have a bad feeling about it."

Elle sighs softly and her eyes grow distant.

"You okay?" I wrap my arms around her waist from behind, resting my cheek against hers.

Elle reaches back and leans into me. "Yeah," she says. "Just tired. Coach gave me three days off. I'm not training until Monday."

I spin her around and pull her close. "For real? Three days with nothing to do? Does that mean we'll actually spend the night together?"

Her smile seems forced, but she hooks her arms around my neck and gives me a kiss. "Yeah, we will."

That evening, Elle falls asleep on the sofa, snoring softly and twitching. I'm happy to see it—I know she's been having trouble sleeping. I pull a blanket over her and kiss her forehead.

I make dinner for the two of us and bring a bottle of wine up from the cellar. I make some more guacamole.

But when Elle wakes up from her nap, she shakes her head at the wine. "I'm good, thanks."

"But you don't have to train tomorrow," I say, pushing the glass closer to her. "Surely you can let loose a little. One glass of wine won't hurt."

"I just feel a bit sick," Elle says with a tight smile. "Can't stomach it right now."

"All right."

She avoids my eye, and I notice she doesn't touch the guacamole. She doesn't even look at it, as if the sight of it makes her ill. Nothing like our first night at the cabin together, when she couldn't get enough of it.

Couldn't get enough of *me*.

Tonight, something is different, and I don't like it.

"Is everything okay, Elle?"

She nods, still not looking at me. "Yeah. I think I just need to lie down. I'm sorry, I wish I was a bit more fun."

I bring her to the bedroom and tuck her in, kissing her forehead. She closes her eyes and turns away from me without another word.

She's just sick or worn out from her intense training. I don't know how she juggles rowing and school on top of seeing me.

There's nothing to worry about. It has nothing to do with me.

That's what I keep telling myself, but I can't help feeling like there's something else going on. Ever since I told her about the dinner party with Dahlia, it almost feels like she's been pulling away from me.

I check on her after an hour or so, and she's fast asleep. Wandering around the lodge is giving me cabin fever, so I jump on my bike outside and take off. It's Thursday evening, which means Bo will have some amateur fights going on at the gym.

I have no desire to go out partying, but I'd like to go somewhere comfortable, familiar, and safe. I miss Bo.

Making my way to the edge of Grimdale, I park my bike a couple of blocks away and walk through the back door of the boxing gym. I can hear the sounds of the fights and a small crowd cheering, and I poke my head around the corner. I take a deep breath, inhaling the familiar smell of the gym equipment and stale sweat.

I've missed it. As much as I haven't needed this particular release for my aggression—I don't have much unreleased aggression anymore—it almost feels like coming home.

"You're not supposed to be here," Bo says, appearing behind me.

I turn to him and grin. "Couldn't stay away."

He nods to one of the kids in the ring. "That's Malik Jones. He's good. Just came in a few weeks ago. Good footwork."

"Fast hands. If he sticks to training, he could be really good."

Bo grunts in agreement and glances at me. "You been keeping out of trouble?"

"Surprisingly, yes," I grin. "Never thought I'd say that and not be lying."

"Who is she?"

"What?"

Bo chuckles and I frown. How could he know about Elle?

The old man nods to his office. "I always said that the only way you'd get rid of that anger in your heart was through the love of a good woman. Come on, I want to give you something."

I follow him to the cramped room, with stacks of yellowing papers and old, broken gym equipment leaning against the walls. Bo's faded leather chair creaks as he sits down, and he pulls out a set of keys that jangle as he finds the right one. Bo unlocks the bottom drawer of his desk and takes out a small, black velvet box.

He pushes it toward me. "Your mother gave me this, back when she brought you in here the first time. She said to give it to you when you were ready. It took a little longer than I thought, but you're ready now."

"My mother?"

"Uh huh." Bo gets a faraway look and gestures for me to open the box.

I flip it open and see my mother's favorite ring. My eyes widen. "She gave you this?"

Bo chuckles. "She did. It was a few months before..." he trains off, and I know he means before she died. "She was a firecracker when she was your age. Good boxer."

"My mother boxed? How have I never heard this before?"

"Why do you think she brought you here?" Bo grins. His eyes get misty as he leans back in his chair. "Incredible woman. She gave that to me for safekeeping. Said it might get lost up at the castle. Told me to give it to you when you had found a woman who tamed your wild side. All I can say is—I hope I get to meet her."

Bo smiles at me, and emotion chokes my throat. I don't know what to say. I look at the ring, and I remember my mother fiddling with it when she was nervous and staring at it when she was lost in thought. It was my mother's mother's ring—and her grandmother before that—a delicate, white gold band with a round emerald stone that reminded me of her eyes. Small diamonds sparkle all around it. I take the ring between my fingers and wipe a tear before it can fall to my cheek.

"I can't believe you knew her that well."

"I did." Bo smiles sadly, and I wonder what really happened between them. He reaches over and squeezes my hand. "She knew you'd be a great King. She used to tell me that you were born to rule, and I think she was right."

If I look at him any longer, I'm going to start crying in earnest. Instead, I put the ring back in the box and slip it into my breast pocket.

"I don't know about that."

"You will," Bo nods. He leans back in his chair and folds his arms over his stomach. "You're a born leader. You just need someone to smooth out the rough edges."

I smile, touching the box against my chest. Elle smooths out my rough edges. She does more than that. She makes me whole, and I already know that she's the only woman who will ever wear my mother's ring.

26

ELLE

I'M PREGNANT.

Ever since those blue lines appeared on the pregnancy test, my mind has been spiraling out of control. I can't even look Charlie in the eye.

Pregnant.

There's a baby growing inside me. I can't wrap my mind around it. An actual, tiny human is being formed at this moment. In my uterus.

When I hear the door close and Charlie's motorcycle drive away, I let out a sigh and roll onto my back. I stare at the ceiling as tears start to fall from my eyes.

This is a monumental disaster.

What was I thinking, not getting the morning after pill? We've used protection since then, but that first night...

I squeeze my eyes shut as a lump grows in my throat. My phone dings. It's Charlie, saying he's going to the boxing gym and he'll be back in an hour.

He's been so considerate lately. Even tonight, he cooked for me and tucked me in. He's so... *loving.*

And I'm carrying his child.

I want to tell Charlie, but every time he looks at me, the words just won't come out. If I tell him, it'll change everything. What if he freaks out? What if he's angry?

What if he wants me to get rid of it? What if he doesn't want to see me anymore?

The thought makes my chest pinch painfully around my heart.

I don't want to lose the Prince.

But I won't give up my baby. I *won't*. There's no way. I can't have a child go through what I went through, living their entire life wondering who their parents are and why they weren't wanted.

No, this child might not have been expected, but it will be wanted. It will be loved, whether or not the Prince wants it, too.

But the thought of telling him, of seeing his reaction... of losing him...

I can't bear it. I curl up into a ball and cry.

Panic starts to snake inside me, needling at all my fears and insecurities. It's all well and good saying that I'll take care of the baby—but how?

I'll lose my scholarship, because I won't be able to compete next year. I won't graduate, which means I can't get a good job.

I'll be a terrible mother. What do I know about being a parent?

How will I provide for the baby? How will I survive?

Squeezing my eyes shut, I twist the blankets in my hands and take a deep breath. It calms me down enough to stay my spiraling thoughts.

My life is royally fucked, which is ironic, considering I've been royally fucked every night for the past two months. My heart starts palpitating and I take a deep breath. I swing my legs over the edge of the bed and stand up, putting a hand to my stomach. Padding to the kitchen, I take one look at the bowl of guacamole and run straight to the bathroom to throw up.

Turns out morning sickness doesn't only happen in the morning.

I cough and sputter as my stomach heaves again, and then I cry into the toilet bowl for a long time.

Picking myself up off the bathroom floor, I brush my teeth and gargle some mouthwash before heading back to bed. I fall into a hazy sort of sleep until Charlie slips in under the covers beside me.

"Hey," I mumble sleepily. "How was the boxing gym?"

"It was great," he says, opening the bedside table drawer, putting something in, and closing it again. "Went to see Bo."

"I thought he'd get shut down if you were seen there."

"He could, but I wasn't there very long. It was good to see him. He's like a father to me."

Charlie wraps his arms around me and pulls me in against his chest. He smells like fresh air and his usual cologne, and I sigh into his skin.

I wish it didn't feel this good to be with him. It would be a hell of a lot easier if he wasn't so perfect.

"How are you feeling?" He strokes my hair and kisses my forehead, and my heart squeezes.

The words won't come. I don't know how to say it.

I mean, I know *how* to say it. I could just blurt out 'I'm pregnant'—but my brain seems to be blocking me from doing that.

Instead, I just sigh. "I feel better now that you're here."

"You still feeling sick? I'll take care of you." He holds me close. Charlie's so tender and loving, and it breaks my heart. It's only a matter of time before I lose him.

Because at the end of the day, I know I'll lose him. I've always known, deep down, that this was never going to work. I held out some sort of hope that we'd be able to take our relationship public, but after the dinner party with Dahlia, those hopes started to fade.

Now that I'm pregnant, I know it's over. For the Crown Prince to have an illegitimate child with a girl from Grimdale...

...that's an even bigger scandal than the Crown Prince hooking up with his governess when he was fifteen. I can't do that to him.

I can't do that to myself, or to my baby. I don't want my kid growing up in the horrible spotlight of scandal, not being given a chance at a decent life.

It has to end between the Prince and me.

But not tonight. Not this weekend. I'll spend these last three days with him, and I'll love him with my entire heart. I'll make love to him, kiss him and hold him and drink everything in... and then I'll say goodbye. I'll finish this year at college and figure something out for next year.

I won't drag him down with me, and I won't hurt my baby.

In that moment, with Prince Charlie's arms wrapped around me, as his breath quiets down and I know he's fallen asleep, I realize that I love him.

God, how I love him.

I love him harder than I've ever loved a man before. He has my heart, my soul, my everything. I curl my fingers into Charlie's chest and kiss his skin. It's stubbly now. He's let his chest hair grow—just like he said he would.

For me.

It's precisely because I love him that I know I can't tell him about the baby. It's because I love him that I need to let him go. This baby will be life-changing for me, but it would be an epic, Kingdom-shattering scandal for him.

And that's not fair for Charlie, or me, or the baby.

I cry silently as Charlie snores beside me. My heart splinters at the thought of losing him, but I know that I'm doing the right thing. Even if I can't have him, I'll have his child to have, and hold, and love—to treat like a little prince or princess.

At the end of the day, that's more important than anything else. I already know that I'll love this baby every bit as much as I love the Prince.

The only way that I can see both the baby and the Prince having a fair chance at life is if I give up this relationship. For my baby, I will. For the Prince to have a chance at being a respected King, I will.

But that doesn't mean I won't cry about it. It doesn't mean it won't hurt like hell.

Charlie mutters something in his sleep and pulls me closer, throwing his leg over mine. I take a deep, shuddering breath and snuggle into his embrace, vowing to enjoy every second of these three days, because I know they'll be the last days I spend with him.

THAT'S EXACTLY what I do. I push the thoughts of the baby aside, and I force myself to get over the fatigue and the nausea, and I enjoy my days off. I haven't had multiple days off in far too long. Charlie and I sleep, and eat, and make love all day long. He takes me out on motorcycle rides. On Sunday, we go to Frank's shelter to help out for a bit before going back to the Valencia's for a family dinner.

They're the happiest and the most heartbreaking days of my life.

When the Prince drops me off at my shabby old house on Sunday evening, I give him a long kiss. This is the moment to say the words. This is the moment to break up with him.

But he flashes a smile at me... and I can't do it. The words stick to my throat and the Prince kisses me again.

I'm too weak.

Instead, I blink back tears and chicken out. "I'm going to be pretty busy these next couple of weeks. I really need to focus on rowing until the regatta."

Charlie grins. "Is that your way of saying you don't want to see me?"

"Not that I don't want to. I can't."

"Fine. I have some court stuff to attend to anyway. But I will be at the regatta with bells on, cheering you on at the finish line."

I force a smile. "Can't wait."

When I get inside the house, I close the door and collapse in a heap on the floor, sobbing. Dahlia runs to me and wraps her arms around me, rocking me gently until I can breathe again.

"It'll be okay," she says, over and over again. "It'll be okay."

And I let myself believe her.

27

CHARLIE

I'm worried about Elle. She seems different when she says goodbye to me. But I also know that the Spring Regatta is coming up, and it's the biggest event of the rowing calendar. She's been working hard for this. I've seen her every morning out on the lake, and in the evenings in the weight room. I've watched her prep her food and avoid parties. She is the exact opposite of how I used to live.

Elle's discipline is awe-inspiring. Over the past two months, I've watched her dial everything in and push her body further than I've ever thought possible.

She's a true athlete, and I have a hell of a lot of respect for her. I don't think I could do what she does. She's completely focused and determined about what she has to do.

And off the water, she's bubbly and bright—or at least she was, up until this week.

I'm just in the middle of sending her a text to tell her how proud I am of her when there's a knock on my bedroom door. My father doesn't wait for my answer before he opens the door and walks in.

"A little privacy, maybe? I could be naked in here. I could have company."

"You haven't had company in here in two months. It's unusual."

"Maybe I'm discovering the virtues of a celibate life."

"Maybe there's a woman you're not telling me about."

I try to keep my face steady, but my jaw ticks. The King notices. He snorts and shakes his head.

"Well, whoever she is, you're going to need to end it. Your time is up. I've chosen for you."

"Fuck you." I pick my phone up again and lay down in bed, ignoring him.

The King chuckles. He steps into my room casting his eye around as if he's a realtor assessing a home for sale.

His eyes land on me. "You think you're above the law, Charlie—above traditions, above me—but you're not. I'm telling you now, I've chosen a wife for you."

"And I'm telling you I won't marry her."

"Aren't you curious as to who she is?"

"Not particularly, no. It doesn't matter."

I can see frustration simmering inside my father, but he does a remarkable job of keeping it contained. He clasps his hands behind his back and takes a few steps further into my room. Stopping at the door to my ensuite, he glances at the locked trash can and swings his eyes back to me.

"I've found the governess." His eyes narrow.

I freeze. She was sent away from here, banished when the scandal broke. If he's found her, it's because he wants leverage over me. He's not ready to give up the Crown, and all this stuff about finding me a wife, about the governess... it's starting to make sense. My father still wants the power, even if the Crown passes to me.

Swinging my eyes up to him, I shrug. "So?"

The King scoffs. "You can pretend that you don't care, but I know that whoever your girlfriend is, she won't like learning about your little sexcapades when you were young."

"She already knows," I shrug. A smile tugs at my lips as I watch my father. Is that all he's got? If he tries to cause another scandal about me and the governess, I'm ready. Ever since I've been with Elle, I've done some thinking. She's helped me shake off the shame of what happened when I was a teenager. She's helped me realize that it wasn't my fault, and that my governess was taking advantage of me.

So, if the King tries to cause a fuss about it? I'm ready. I'll take all the slings and arrows that the press can throw at me, and I'll tell them the truth about everything that happened.

If that's all my father has over me as leverage, he has nothing. The governess doesn't hold any power over me anymore.

The King's lips twitch into a mirthless smile. "So there is a woman? I wasn't sure, but you've just confirmed it."

I blink.

Shit.

"Who is she?"

"Why do you care? You've already written her off."

"You're too much like your mother, Charles. You don't understand the importance of traditions. This Kingdom is built on tradition. We have customs that go back hundreds of years, and the people respect us because we respect the throne."

"No, the people respect us because they think we care about them. And I actually do. If that makes me too much like my mother? Well, good. I'd rather be like her than you."

"You're a fool."

"Is that the only reason you're here? To threaten to tell the world about the governess again? You'll have to do better than that, Father. Take the wife you've chosen and shove her up your ass."

He says nothing, only stares at me for a few moments and huffs. I look at my bedroom door, where Talin appears from the shadows. He bows to my father, who stalks out of my room and slams the door behind him.

My blood boils. I stare at the closed door as my muscles tense, rage growing inside me as I replay our conversation over and over again in my head.

My own father is threatening me.

At least now I know why. He doesn't want to give up the throne, or any bit of his power. Once I'm named the official heir, my word will carry more weight. My father needs to make sure that I'm still under his thumb.

He's trying to do it through my wife, and through any bit of dirt that he can gather on me.

Well, joke's on him, because I'm not marrying whoever he's chosen, and scandals no longer bother me. I'm a new man, and I know what I want.

I want a certain tall, brown-haired and brown-eyed rower with a sharp tongue and a banging body. I clutch my phone and scroll through my photos, smiling at all the ones we've taken together.

She's the one. No question about it.

I was worried about my father before, but now I know he's got nothing on me. If that little threat is the worst he's got, then I'm free to show Elle off to the world.

After the Spring Regatta, when Elle wins her medal and her prize money, I'm going to make her my wife.

28

ELLE

FOR THE NEXT WEEK, I avoid Prince Charlie. I'm too busy with rowing, I tell him.

It's mostly true. The lead up to the regatta is intense. I'm in my peak week of training, making sure my nutrition, sleep, and training are dialed in perfectly.

A small tendril of doubt snakes through me as I push myself during my last few training sessions before the regatta. Maybe I shouldn't be doing this. What if it's bad for the baby?

But I quash the thought as soon as it enters my head. If Serena Williams can win the Australian Open while two months pregnant, I can win the Farcliff Regatta. I've worked too hard, and for too long to give up now. I've spent hours on the water. I've given up parties, and late nights, and every-thing else that a normal college kid would enjoy.

Everything in my life has led up to this moment. Last year, I didn't qualify.

This year, I'm going to win.

Baby or not. Impending breakup or not.

I think Charlie understands that, because he doesn't push

to see me. He sends me texts and pictures, telling me he's proud of me, but he gives me space.

Damn it, he's so thoughtful and so easy to love. If he was crowding me or putting too much pressure on me, I could get mad and push him away. I could give myself an excuse to break it off.

But he's perfect, and I can't.

So I just do what I do best. I focus on rowing.

Coach Bernard is happy with my last few sessions. My nutrition is perfect, and I'm finally sleeping a bit better. In a way, it feels good to have the regatta to focus on.

Whenever I start freaking out about the baby, I put that energy into rowing. If I feel sad about the Prince, I row. My heart, my soul, my prayers all go into the competition.

Charlie seems to be in good spirits. His texts and phone calls are loving and positive, and it makes me wonder if it only seems that way because my mind is deep in a negative space. Does he seem happier than before, or am I just more sad?

Dahlia goes with me to the doctor, and I learn that I'm perfectly healthy, and my pregnancy is completely normal so far.

Late at night, when I can't row or run or train, I lay there with my arm curled around my stomach and I cry.

THE DAY OF THE REGATTA, I wake up full of nervous energy. My entire day is planned out to the minute. I already have my clothes laid out for the day, and all my pre- and post-race snacks are packed. My meals are prepped and ready, and I chow down a hearty breakfast before heading to the lakeshore.

Olivia and Marielle's snide comments don't even bother

me. They have their events, and I have mine. Their opinions mean nothing—not today.

This is what I live for. Today is competition day, and I'm here to win.

I put everything else out of my mind. Right now, it doesn't matter.

Tomorrow, I'll deal with my future, but today, I just need to win this race. It's just me and the water.

An hour before my event, I sit on the lakeside and close my eyes. I visualize myself crossing the finish line. I imagine the crowd waiting and cheering, the smell of the water and the trees, the feel of the oars in my hands and the boat beneath me. I visualize every single detail until I've already won the event once in my mind.

Then, I get up, and I'm ready to do it again—for real this time.

Coach Bernard is there, giving me last minute encouragement, but I hardly hear him. This is what I'm made to do. I brush my hand over my stomach before I get in my shell, closing my eyes once more.

This is for you, kid.

Getting in the water feels like coming home. My muscles are warm, and my heart is thumping with a strong, steady heartbeat.

A smile drifts over my lips, and I run my hands over my oars. As I make my way to my starting position, my body and mind feel completely aligned. I'm ready.

When the gun goes off, I row.

No, I don't row. I *fly*. My strokes are smooth, cutting through the water like butter. I'm a dancer, floating along the surface as each stroke brings me closer to the finish line. Closer to my destiny.

My muscles burn and my lungs scream, and I push harder. Faster.

It feels exactly as it did in my mind. I smell the lake. I hear the oars dipping into the water. When I get closer to the finish line, I hear the excited crowd and the announcer booming over the loudspeaker.

I close my eyes and I pull.

My legs are about to give out and my lungs need more oxygen. My shoulders and arms and in pain. I reach into that pain, tasting it on my tongue as I pull the oars through the water again, and again, and again.

Pain tastes good. It tastes like victory.

The coppery tang of blood fills my mouth and I know I'm reaching my limit. I squeeze my eyes shut again and think of my baby. I'm doing this for my child. I'll win, just to show my kid that anything is possible. I need that prize money more than ever—but maybe more importantly, I need to prove to myself that I can do it. That I'm worthy. That I can win something of my own merit, based on my own strengths and off the back of my own hard work.

My child will be able to look at me and be proud of knowing where they came from.

The sounds of the crowd roar in my ears as I pull the oars through the water one last time. My eyes are still closed, my breath ragged as my muscles scream in sweet, glorious agony.

When I open my eyes again, I'm past the finish line, and my name is flashing at the top of the big screen.

I won.

I fucking *won*.

A scream rips through me. It tears through my chest and burns my throat as I roar. I lift my arms up over my head and yell so loud it hurts as tears stream down my cheeks.

It's the sound that only an athlete knows. I scream for

every hour that I've spent on this lake, for every extra training session, and for everything I've given up. I scream for my baby, and for the end of my relationship with the Prince.

Pumping my arms above my head, I look over at the crowd on the shore and see Prince Charlie on his feet, whooping and hollering for me. He's beaming.

Dahlia was right—he loves me. Of course she was right. He's stupidly in love with me, just as I am with him. I'll never love anyone as much as I love him. His strength, his humor, his tattoos, his energy.

His tenderness. His passion.

I smile at him, and for the briefest of moments, I'm truly, completely happy.

Then my stomach churns.

In front of the entire royal family, all of Farcliff, and all the visiting colleges... I lean over the side of my boat and puke. The movement makes my shell heave sideways and it moves too suddenly for me to right it again.

My arms flail, my knees buck. Another panicked scream slips through my lips.

Then, right after the happiest moment of my life, I capsize my boat and fall headlong into Farcliff Lake.

29

CHARLIE

I DON'T EVEN REALIZE I'm running until my steps shake the pier with a dull *thud-thud-thud*. Vaguely, I hear cameras flashing behind me, and someone shouting at me to stop. An arm tries to grab me, but I dodge out of the way.

My only focus is Elle. The instant she disappeared under the water, I went from elated to panicked. I launch myself off the end of the pier and dive into the murky, cold water of Farcliff Lake.

It takes more than a few powerful strokes to get me close to her boat. She went under near the center of the lake, where the water is deep and black. I need to get to her.

If she doesn't come back up...

A million horrible thoughts cross my mind. I poke my head out of the water with the intention of filling my lungs to dive right back down when I see the vessel right itself. Elle's head pops up above the other side of her boat.

Her eyes land on me as I tread water.

"Charlie?"

"You're alive," I pant, swimming the rest of the way to her.

She laughs. "Uh, yeah. What are you doing in here? Did you jump in?"

"I thought..." My eyebrows draw together. "Uh, I saw you throw up and then you fell in and I was worried... Are you okay?"

We both hang onto either side of her scull, staring at each other. The water is cold—it's the middle of April, and the lake is still freezing. It's starting to shock my body, and I try to keep moving as much as possible as my limbs get heavy and my breath slows down. "You good?" I ask.

Elle's face falls. She swallows, averting her eyes.

"What's wrong, Elle?"

She still won't look at me. A motor revs in the distance, and I know that the rescue team will be here soon.

"Elle?" My heart skips a beat and worry starts wriggling in my heart. Why won't she look at me? What is she hiding? Why does she still want to avoid me if the race is over? She won—she should be happy!

"I'm pregnant."

Her eyes—big and brown and full of pain—sweep up to meet mine, and I freeze.

Blame the cold water, if you like. Blame shock. Whatever it is, it seizes my muscles and makes my jaw go slack. She stares at me with her eyebrows drawn together, and I know I need to say something. Anything.

But I can't.

The rescue boat arrives to pick me up. Elle lifts herself up into her shell in one smooth motion and nods to the rescue team, who let her paddle back to safety on her own.

And I have to sit in the power boat, watching.

She still won't look at me.

We arrive at the pier amidst cameras and the clamoring of

reporters. They push Elle and I together and snap photos of us. I force a smile.

Elle doesn't. She mumbles something about hypothermia and pushes past everyone, angling toward her team. One of the coaches drapes a blanket over her shoulders, narrowing his eyes at me. I still haven't said a word. I'm led away in the opposite direction.

"What was that about?" My brother Gabriel arches an eyebrow. "I've never seen you run that fast in my life."

"Or swim in waters that weren't tropical," Damon grins.

"She looked like she was in trouble."

"So?" He frowns. Cameras are still flashing. My thoughts are spinning.

Pregnant?

I can't get my head around it. I swing my eyes over to Elle again, but she's surrounded by her teammates and isn't looking my way. Neville appears at my side and leads me away to get warmed up and changed.

I should have said something. I should have reached over and grabbed her hand. I should have reacted.

But I didn't.

I froze, and now she thinks I'm angry. Thoughts fly around my head like dead leaves in the wind. I put one foot in front of the other, walking mechanically back to my chambers.

Am I angry?

I strip my soaking wet clothes off and walk into my shower, trying to figure out exactly how I feel. My eye catches on my lockable trash can, and my jaw ticks.

This is exactly what I wanted to avoid for my entire adult life, but it doesn't feel bad. It doesn't feel wrong.

It feels... great, actually.

She's pregnant. I'm going to be a father. A smile drifts over my lips and I start laughing to myself.

Elle is carrying *my* child.

Images flash through my mind. My kid—son or daughter, it doesn't matter—growing up in the castle. Elle, happy and glowing as she chases after them. Maybe she's pregnant with our second.

The feeling hits me like a lightning bolt. *Happiness.*

I want that. I want *her.*

The shower steams up and my muscles start to work again. I flex my hands and work the knots out of my neck, and I laugh again.

She's pregnant with *our* child.

As my body temperature rises, my smile widens. I wash myself off and get out of the shower, rushing to find some dry clothes. I need to find her. I need to tell her, to marry her, to scream to the world that I'm in love with her.

But I don't make it that far. Just outside my door, Talin is waiting to drag me to my father.

"I'm busy," I say, trying to brush him off.

"Your father requests your presence." Talin's eyes narrow as three security guards step out of the shadows. My first instinct is to fight, but they puff their chests out and I pause.

I could take one of them, sure—but three?

A small smirk appears on Talin's lips. He knows he's won. I slump my shoulders and follow him down to one of the castle's reception rooms. Every step makes my anger ratchet up. When the door opens onto one of the castle's immaculately decorated formal reception rooms, my blood boils.

My father isn't alone. He's with Olivia Brundle, of all people. She looks like a Barbie doll, and not in a good way. Olivia pushes her plastic chest out at me and all I can think of is Elle's glorious natural one.

Standing up, Olivia plasters a smile on her face.

My father clears his throat. "Charles, you know Miss Brundle, your betrothed."

"My *what?*"

Olivia's smile trembles a touch, but to her credit, it doesn't drop. She's been well-trained—just like a dog.

The King rolls his eyes and waves for the doors behind me to be closed. "Sit down, son. It's time that we made this official." His beady little eyes narrow, and I know I can't fight this right now.

So, I sit down. Olivia settles in her seat again, folding her hands on her lap—just as she was programmed to do.

I miss Elle's spontaneity, her uniqueness. I miss how casual she's always been with me. This charade—with royal manners and traditions—it drives me nuts.

I need Elle's realness.

Olivia bats her eyelashes at me. "I saw what you did at the regatta. It was very brave of you to jump in like that. I'm on the team as well. It made me wish I'd capsized at the finish line." She giggles coquettishly, and it bores me.

"Brave... or stupid," the King mumbles. "You could have gotten hypothermia."

I swing my eyes from one to the other, not knowing what to say. They're both acting like this is completely normal. Like my father didn't just drag me in here by force and command me to marry this chick.

A couple of months ago, I'd have played along and probably fucked her. Hell, I might already have done, I can't remember.

But now?

Fuck no.

"Do you know Elle?" Olivia's lips pinch when she says the name, and the skin around her eyes tightens ever so slightly.

"Excuse me?"

"Just the way you jumped in... it looked like you really cared about her."

A tense silence fills the room, and all I want to do is jump up and scream, *Yes! Yes, I know her. I'm in love with her, and I'm not fucking marrying you.*

But I can't. If I say anything about her, I'm putting Elle in the crosshairs. My father knows I'm seeing someone, but as far as I'm aware, he doesn't know who.

Based on the way Olivia was asking about me and Elle, it's obvious they aren't friends.

I can't put Elle in danger. I can't admit that I know her, because then she'll become a target of whatever fucked-up ideas my father has. I don't know what he's capable of.

So, I pull a Judas and deny it. "No, never seen her. She just looked like she was in trouble."

"How brave of you," Olivia smiles, but I can see the jealousy bubbling just under the surface. That's a great quality in a fiancée I've never met before. She's already feeling possessive.

"Well," I say, pushing myself to my feet. "I was on my way out. Nice to meet you, Miss Brundle. Father," I nod. I turn to the door, but my father stops me.

"Where could you possibly have to go that's more interesting than here? The beautiful and talented Olivia came to the castle specifically to ask if you were all right. Show some decency."

I make it to the doors, but they're locked from the outside. My jaw ticks. My father has locked me in this room with him and Olivia Brundle, and now I have no choice but to play along.

Frustration builds inside me until I feel like I'm going to

explode. I turn slowly, stalking back to the chair that I just vacated.

Olivia clears her throat and stands up, turning toward the King. "Charlie and I are so pleased that you'll announce our betrothal today, Your Majesty." She puts her hand on my shoulder and I flinch, but her fingers dig in and hang on.

I brush her off and she takes a step back from me, her eyebrows arched in surprise.

I turn to my father, my anger quickly turning to rage. "Today?"

My father grins. "Of course. What better day than today? It's the Spring Regatta. The stage is set up already."

"Father," I say, forcing my face to stay steady and my voice to remain calm. "May I have a word in private?"

"I don't think that's necessary," he says, waving a hand. "We've had plenty of time to discuss this." He pulls out a white envelope from his breast pocket and tosses it over to me. It lands on my lap, and I stare at it for a moment. My father has a triumphant grin on his face, and dread trips down my spine and settles in the pit of my stomach.

I've seen his face like this before, and only when he knows he's won something. And right now, I'm the poor schmuck who's just lost.

With trembling hands, I open the envelope and pull out some papers.

They're medical records—more specifically, they're Elle's medical records. I skim them and my heart drops out of my ass. I read about Elle's recent visit to the doctor, where her pregnancy was confirmed.

Perfectly healthy, apparently, and not at all secret from my father.

The King not only knows about Elle, he knows about the

baby, too. He probably knew she was pregnant before I did. My jaw clenches, and I look up at him. He laughs and presses a button on the side table. The doors fly open. Waiters flood in carrying trays of champagne as if there's anything to celebrate.

My father and Olivia pretend like they haven't just ambushed me with this, clinking their glasses together. I stare at the paper again.

Olivia smiles at me, and a part of me dies.

The governess might not be meaningful leverage for my father, but this is. My father has me right where he wants me, and there's nothing I can do about it.

30

ELLE

THE PROBLEM with having a secret relationship is that when it inevitably falls apart, there's no one there to comfort you. I watch the Prince walk away and my heart breaks. I see the shock on his face when I tell him about the baby. I've seen his lockable garbage cans. I know about his past with his governess.

I can put two and two together—this baby isn't wanted.

But seeing the look on his face still hurts like hell.

It takes me almost an hour to warm up. By that time, the Prince has disappeared, and the medal ceremony is underway.

With a thermal blanket over my shoulders, I accept my gold medal. Typically, it would be the King who presents them. He's nowhere to be found, so Prince Damon hooks it over my head instead.

"Congrats, Elle," he says with a wink. "You deserve it."

"Thanks."

"Tell Dahlia I said hello."

I manage to nod. "Yeah. Yeah, okay." My eyes scan the Royal Box and the crowd, but I can't see Charlie anywhere. I open my mouth to ask Prince Damon where he's gone, but the Prince has already been whisked away by his handlers.

Frank and Tina come rushing toward me as soon as the ceremony is over. Tina wraps me in a tight hug as they both congratulate me. I plaster a smile on my face, but I can't quite make it convincing enough.

"Honey, is everything okay?"

I nod. "Still a bit cold, that's all."

Dahlia appears, wearing pure-white pants and a pink faux fur jacket. Her multicolored hair is braided in two French braids on either side of her head. Somehow, she makes everything look sophisticated, cool, and way trendier than I'll ever be.

My best friend wraps her arms around me. "Congrats, Elle," she says. "How are you feeling?"

I give her a sad smile and understanding flashes across her face.

"You want me to take you home?"

I nod, turning to Frank and Tina. "Thank you so much for coming. Do you mind if we postpone dinner until tomorrow?"

"Of course, honey," Tina smiles. She wraps me in another motherly hug, and it takes all my self-control not to break down crying.

I wish I could tell them everything that's happened since the Prince's Ball. I wish I could tell them about the baby, about the Prince, and about the fact that I'm completely freaking out about everything in my life right now.

Instead, I just pull away and let Dahlia take me home. We drive her orange Jeep back to our run-down house, and I take a deep breath the moment we arrive. At least I'm home, now. Away from prying eyes so I can wallow in peace.

She leads me to the couch and drapes a blanket over me,

and then disappears into the kitchen. I lay there, unable to think or move or feel.

When Dahlia reappears, she has a pot of tea, two boxes of cookies, and a bag of chips. She plops herself down on the couch and grabs a cookie before handing me the rest of the box.

"How are you feeling?"

"I don't know." I snort bitterly. "He doesn't want the baby."

"You told him?"

"Yeah, in the water. I just blurted it out."

Dahlia looks at me and exhales slowly. "And he told you he didn't want it?"

"He didn't say anything."

"Well, don't panic. It's cold in Farcliff Lake, maybe he was hypothermic. He was probably in shock. He might come around."

"If he wanted a baby, he wouldn't need to 'come around', Dahlia."

She pinches her lips and reaches for another cookie. "Don't panic."

"Easier said than done."

"At least you won."

"Yeah, go me," I scoff, shaking my head. "Fat load of good that'll do when I'm kicked out of school next year."

"Okay, stop." Dahlia turns to me and puts her hands on my lap. "You need to stop freaking out. We will figure this out."

"How? I still have another year of college that I can't afford without this scholarship. I'll lose that, and then I won't be able to finish my degree. On top of that, I'll have a baby to deal with."

"What about summer classes? Night classes? Part-time?

You can work and study. I'll help. I'll loan you money. The Prince will pay! It's his kid, too!"

Tears sting my eyes and I shake my head. "I don't know about that."

"Listen to me, Elle. This *will* work out. You want this baby, yeah?"

"Yes, of course I do." I put my hand to my stomach. "I want to be the best mother I possibly can be, but I don't know how to do that."

"I think most mothers feel that way," Dahlia smiles. "Don't forget that you have me, you have the Valencias, and you have the Prince. You're not alone. We'll help you, and we'll figure it all out. Takes a village, right? We're your village. Right here."

I take a deep breath and let her words sink in. Nodding, I let a tear fall from my eye. "You won't abandon me?"

Dahlia laughs. "No, you're stuck with me." She grabs the TV remote and clicks it on. "Come on, let's watch something trashy and forget the world exists."

I nod, settling into the sofa. My whole body is exhausted from the race, from capsizing, from the shock of telling Charlie about the baby. My eyelids feel heavy and I sink down into the cushions as I make myself comfortable.

Dahlia finds something for us to watch and I'm almost asleep when the show cuts out.

"*Breaking news from Farcliff Castle,*" the man on the screen proclaims. "*We have just received word that Prince Charlie is engaged.*"

I sit bolt upright, grabbing the remote from Dahlia and turning the volume way up.

"*After years of speculation, the Prince has announced his betrothal to Oliva Brundle, daughter of Marcus Brundle. Olivia is a successful political science student and member of Farcliff University's rowing team..."*

A strangled sort of gasp escapes my lips as my eyes widen. "Olivia?"

Dahlia doesn't even have a way of explaining this away. She can't calm me down. My whole body is shaking. We both stay glued to the screen, where the King, Olivia, and Charlie appear at a castle balcony. The Prince and Olivia are holding hands, and they lift their clasped hands up above their heads. Olivia is beaming. Charlie looks sick.

"What... how..." I gulp down a breath as my stomach rolls. I'm going to throw up.

"Don't panic, Elle, we don't know..."

I run to the bathroom, but I don't quite make it in time. I throw up all over the bathroom floor, and then I collapse beside the mess and start sobbing. My head is spinning. My stomach hurts. My heart is broken.

The Prince is engaged to someone other than me.

Even worse, he's engaged to Olivia fucking Brundle, the girl who has tortured me every day for the past three years.

No wonder he didn't want the baby. No wonder he reacted like that.

Dahlia stands at the doorway and sighs. She crouches down beside me and brushes my hair out of my face and then disappears for a moment. When she comes back, she has a glass of water and a roll of paper towels. I reach for both, but she keeps the paper towels.

"I'll clean this up," she says gently. "You just wash your mouth and get into bed."

"It's okay, I can—"

"Clean your mouth and get into bed," she says, her voice stern. "Go."

I don't have the energy to protest. I'm still trying to wrap my head around what's happened. I won the regatta, which should be the happiest day of my life.

Instead, it's the worst.

The Prince is getting married.

He knows I'm pregnant, and yet he still agreed to marry someone else.

I brush my teeth and stumble into bed, grateful that Dahlia is here. I lay on my side, eyes wide open, as the TV anchor's voice replays in my head over and over again.

That's why Charlie reacted the way he did. He knew he was getting married to someone else, and I just made his life a hell of a lot more complicated.

Didn't I say this would end with a long, hard fall? Well, turns out it's a short, devastating one. I knew it would hurt, but I had no idea it would feel like this.

Squeezing my eyes shut, my chest squeezes so tightly that I feel my heart splinter within it. I *knew* this would happen. From the beginning of my relationship with the Prince, I knew it would end in disaster.

I set myself up for heartbreak, yet I still ran head-first into it. I dove in the deep end without thinking twice, and now I have no future, no money, and no degree.

All I have is an unplanned baby and a broken heart.

I clutch my stomach as the tears start to fall from my eyes. No matter what, I refuse to think of this baby as a curse. Rocking back and forth, I focus on the life that's growing inside me.

Even if the Prince doesn't want me or our baby, I know what I want. Even if it means it'll take me ten years to finish my degree. Even if I have to live with the Valencias until I'm forty, if it means I have to work four jobs.

I'll do it.

No one can take this baby away from me, and no one can

make me love it any less. I'm terrified and heartbroken, but I've never been more sure of anything in my life.

The Prince may not want this baby, but I do.

So, as my heart shatters, I focus on my child. This kid is like a pulsing light inside me—the one thing that I can hang on to, the one thing that will bring me joy when everything else in my life turns to ash.

31

CHARLIE

AS OLIVIA LIFTS my arm up in the air and flashes a smile at the crowd below, my stomach does another horrible flip. I wonder what the headlines would say if I threw up right now?

PRINCE CHARLIE THROWS UP ON WIFE-TO-BE
DOES PRINCE CHARLIE PUKE OF HAPPINESS... OR DISGUST?
ENGAGEMENT INDUCES PROJECTILE VOMITING

Maybe it would be worth it just to wipe that triumphant smirk off Olivia's face. But then my thoughts turn to Elle, and that medical record that my father somehow acquired.

Is Elle seeing this on TV? Does she believe it? Does she think I don't want the baby?

I don't know how I'll do it yet, but I need to get out of this. I need to find a way to get my father to release me from this engagement.

If I walk away from Olivia Brundle, my father will refuse to name me his heir and he'll release the information about Elle's pregnancy. I wouldn't mind that, really—but I know it would be crushing for Elle. The press can be vicious, and I don't want to put her in that position. I don't want to put our baby in that position.

Not only that—if I walk away now, I'm putting Damon or Gabriel in line for the throne, and I know they don't want it. Damon would do it, sure, and he'd be a good King, but I'd be making him give up his dreams for me. I can't do that to my brother.

But if I agree to marry Olivia, I'm turning my back on Elle —and our baby.

I disengage my hand from Olivia's and turn back to the door. As soon as I'm inside again, I nod to the guards at the balcony doors. "Close the balcony doors."

"Charlie..." Olivia starts to say before I raise a hand to stop her.

"Don't call me that."

"Excuse me? What am I supposed to call you?" She laughs, frowning. Does she still not understand that my father is using us both? Does she think I *want* this?

Olivia takes a step toward me. "We're engaged to be married. Do you really think it's appropriate to call you by your formal title?"

"I think it's appropriate to treat me like your fucking Prince," I answer, turning to face her. My shoulders stiffen and my face gets darker. Olivia takes a step back, her arms falling to her sides.

My father is already making comments about little heirs, and the thought of having sex with this woman is repulsive to me. No part of me wants to touch her.

She's an attractive woman, sure, but she's not for me. She's not Elle.

My father enters the room, smirking. "That wasn't so hard, now, was it? I'm glad you came around."

"I did it for Elle and my brothers, not for you. This isn't over."

"But you did it," the King says, stepping up to me. His chest puffs up and I resist the urge to punch him in his smug fucking face. He thinks he's won, but I'll find a way out of this. I have to.

As if he reads my mind, he starts to chuckle. "There's no slithering your way out of this one, Charles. You will marry Miss Brundle, and you'll make lots of happy little heirs. You'll forget about the girl in the lake."

My eyes narrow. "Don't—"

"Don't what? Hurt her? Don't give me a reason to hurt her." He scoffs, shaking his head. "After that little stunt with Dahlia Raventhal, I had Talin keep an eye on you. You've always liked a woman who doesn't know her place, haven't you?"

I know he's talking about my mother, and how she'd speak up for the people of Grimdale and the less fortunate of Farcliff. She wasn't the smiling arm candy he'd wanted, and he hated her for it. I'm starting to wonder if Tabitha Raventhal's accusations had any truth to them after all.

Now, my father's making sure that I play by his rules.

The King takes another step toward me, his chest puffing out like a gorilla. "If I even get a whiff of scandal from you, Charles, I won't name you my heir. You'll be nobody. Try making your way in the world out there when you aren't the Crown Prince—I dare you. You need me just as much as I need you, and for once, I expect you to obey."

"Fuck you."

The King laughs. "Oh, and Charlie? The cabinet is meeting about the Farcliff Dam Project next week. As far as you're concerned, it's a great thing for the Kingdom, understood? No grandstanding about fucking Grimdale."

"What? What does this have to do with anything? It's not a great thing for the Kingdom. It'll displace twelve million people from Grimdale to... where? Where will they go?"

"One word out of your insolent mouth, and that little medical record gets leaked."

My chest heaves. Anger threatens to explode out of me in all directions, and I can't take it anymore. I push past the King and knock a guard to the ground as I storm out. I hear my father call out to let me go, and I hate that he has this much control over me. He has to hold our own guards back from me.

As soon as I'm out of the room, I jog down the castle hallways toward the garage. I need to see Elle. I need to talk to her and to make sure she's okay. I need to explain—but how? How can I explain this? How can I make this right?

I jump on my bike and fly down the roads. My hands grip the motorcycle as I accelerate faster, faster, faster. I run a red light and a chorus of honks follows me down the road.

I don't care. I need to see the woman I love.

Practically crashing the bike outside her house, I skid to a stop and jump off it, running to the front door. My fist bangs on it as I yell through the window. The door shakes in its frame as I pound it harder.

"Elle! Elle! Answer the door." I try the doorknob and finding it open, I rush inside. Dahlia appears in the hallway and says something I don't hear. I burst through Elle's bedroom door and find her huddled in bed, crying.

She scrambles up when I enter, wiping her face and clutching the blankets to her chest. "Charlie—Your Highness —what are you doing here?"

"I need to talk to you." I sit down on the bed, reaching for her. She shies away from me and my hand freezes in midair. I let it drop. "I... How are you feeling?"

"Fantastic."

I almost laugh. Even at a time like this, she's biting and sarcastic and everything I want in a woman.

I take a deep breath and stare into her eyes, hoping, praying that she understands. "Elle, I don't want to marry that girl. My father ambushed me. He knows about the baby. He somehow got a hold of your medical record and he knows you're pregnant. I'll find a way out of this, Elle, I promise. I want you. Not her. Not Olivia."

Elle stares at me for a moment before dropping her eyes. She brushes another tear away and then takes a deep breath. When she lifts her face back up to meet my gaze, her eyes are so full of sadness it knocks me back.

Despite the pain in her gaze, her voice is strong. "It was never going to work between us, Charlie. We both knew it all along."

"You're carrying my child."

"Yes."

"Doesn't that mean anything?"

"It means everything, Charlie." Her voice cracks. She reaches over and clasps my hand. "But you're from a different world than I am. I'll never belong up there at the castle."

A lump forms in my throat. She's pushing me away. She doesn't want to fight this—not like I want to fight it. She's letting my father win. "No, Elle, it's not like that."

"It's exactly like that. You're engaged to be married, Charlie." Her voice chokes and she takes a deep, shuddering breath. "We both knew this would happen. We both knew you'd have to marry someone suitable, otherwise you're handing the responsibility over to your brothers. We've talked about this. I'm not fit to be a Queen."

"You are." Tears spill onto my cheeks and I squeeze her

hand. "You'd be a better Queen than any of those 'suitable' girls, Elle."

She laughs bitterly. "Maybe so, but that's not how the world sees it." She puts a hand to her stomach. "We'll be fine, the baby and me. I'll figure it out."

"No." I shake my head. "No, I refuse to accept this. You can't just shut me out like that. That's *my* child growing inside you. I want it. I want *you*."

"Do you, though? I saw your reaction at the lake." She shakes her head. "Charlie, think about it. It's too complicated. I'll never be your wife. I'll just be a scandal waiting to erupt. I'll never be accepted into the royal family, and I'll never be Queen. You shouldn't be here. I'm just leverage for your father to use against you...or whoever else wants to hurt you."

"Elle..."

"Just go, Charlie. There's no future between us. There never was." She turns her head away from me and all I want to do is jump and scream. I want to make her see that there is a future. There has to be. Without her...

...there's nothing.

"There can be a future." My voice breaks on the last word. I refuse to let go of her hand. She's cold and trembling, and I know she doesn't mean what she's saying. She can't. I won't accept it. I won't walk away from her.

Elle shakes her head but doesn't pull her hand away. Her eyes meet mine and my heart breaks.

She takes a deep breath. "How? How can there be a future? Are you going to announce that you're marrying your pregnant girlfriend? Who's not only from Grimdale, but she doesn't even know who her real parents are? How would you get your father to agree to that? Huh? There's no way, Charlie. This has gone on long enough. It's time for us to be honest about this."

She pulls her hand away and turns her head, squeezing her eyes shut. I already know this is over. I know she's right, but I can't just walk away.

"Elle..."

"I care about you," she says softly, not meeting my eye. "You've given me so much that I never thought I'd have. You made me feel beautiful and special... thank you."

"Don't say that, Elle. You *are* beautiful and special and I lov—"

"You should go." She lays down with her back to me, pulling her blankets up to her chin. "Go and be with your fiancée. Do your duty. Be a King."

"I don't want to be King, Elle. I want you. I want our baby."

She turns to look at me, her cheeks soaked with tears. I try to brush them away, but she stops my hand. "It doesn't matter what you want, Charlie. Don't you understand? It doesn't matter what either of us want. This is the world we live in. You're the Crown Prince, and I'm nobody. It wasn't meant to be."

"Don't say that, Elle, I—"

"Just go. Please, Charlie. Don't make this harder than it has to be."

The door opens and Dahlia appears. She nods to me and I freeze. I can't go. I can't leave her. I can't walk away—but I know she's right.

I was born into a life of privilege, and that comes with responsibility. My life was never my own. My mother taught me that. Elle understands it, and it's time for me to get it through my own thick head.

I can never have Elle, because she doesn't come from the same world as I do. If I choose her, I turn my back on my brothers, on my Kingdom, on my duty. If I choose her, I might even be putting her and our baby in danger.

I don't know what my father is capable of, but I do know that he's a vindictive, power-hungry piece of shit. The only way I can protect Elle is by turning my back on her.

When I walk out of that room, I leave something behind. A piece of my heart stays lodged with Elle, and I know I'll never get it back. For as long as I live, my heart will never be whole again.

She may be right—I need to be who I was born to be— but that doesn't mean I'll ever be the same. When Dahlia closes the front door behind me, the lock slides shut and I know I've lost the only person I've ever truly loved.

32

ELLE

I KNOW that was the right thing to do, but it feels awful. Every word that came out of my mouth when Charlie was sitting on my bed sounded wrong. I wanted to take them all back and throw my arms around him, pretending that it would work out.

It won't, though.

We can't be together. It's time we admitted it to ourselves —it was never meant to be. I rub my hand over my stomach and squeeze my eyes shut, curling myself into a tight ball.

"At least you gave me this baby, Charlie," I whisper. Even if I can't have the Prince, I can have his child. It's terrifying, and I know it won't be easy—but it feels right.

All the love I have inside me and all the love that Charlie showed me, I can give it to this baby. I'll love my child with my entire heart and soul.

I hear Charlie's motorcycle rev outside and then he drives away.

It's over.

I thought my heart was already broken, but hearing him drive away shatters it all over again. I roll onto my back and inhale, but I can't get enough air into my lungs. My face twists into an ugly sob, but no sound comes out. My body convulses and I curl my hands into the blankets as my whole body is racked with sharp, piercing daggers of pain.

He's gone, and I know it's forever.

Dahlia's footsteps stop outside my door and a soft knock follows. "You okay?"

I can't breathe, so I can't answer. Dahlia knows. She comes in and wraps her arms around me, rocking me back and forth as I cry harder than I ever have before. I shake and sob until her shirt is drenched with my tears.

"You did the right thing, Elle. I'm proud of you."

I tremble and snort, wiping my tears and snot and grief on the blankets. "I wish... I don't know what I wish. I wish I wasn't from Grimdale."

"If you weren't exactly who you are, the Prince wouldn't have loved you," she said softly. "You are who you are for a reason, Elle, and I don't ever want you to change."

"It just sucks."

Dahlia chuckles, stroking my hair as I lay back down on the pillows. "Yes, it sucks. A lot of things suck."

I sniffle. "He wanted the baby."

"Of course he did, silly. He loves you."

"Don't say that, Dahlia."

"It's the truth."

"I don't want to hear it. It makes it hurt so much more that we can't be together."

Dahlia sighs and lays down in bed beside me. We both stare at the ceiling in silence. "Maybe if we get rid of the King, he won't need that stupid heir naming ceremony, and Charlie can choose you instead of Olivia Brundle."

"*Get rid of*? Are you suggesting murder? Regicide?"

Dahlia sighs. "No, I mean... I don't know what I mean. I don't want to kill anyone. This isn't right, though."

I laugh, and Dahlia grins. She elbows me. "It was just an idea."

"Not the kind of idea I want to entertain. I don't want to live the rest of my life in prison."

She sighs. "I know. It just seems so wrong that you can't be together because of some stupid tradition, and because the King doesn't want to give up the throne when he's supposed to."

"We can't change it, Dahl. It is what it is."

"It's the twenty-first century. We shouldn't need stupid betrothal traditions. Everyone should be able to choose who they want to marry. You, me, the Prince—everyone."

"But we can't."

We're silent for a while, and I feel empty. Dahlia turns on her side and glances down at my stomach. "What does it feel like?"

"What, pregnancy?"

"Yeah."

I shrug. "I get nauseous sometimes. My boobs hurt."

"I can't believe you won the regatta while two months pregnant."

I grin. "I know."

"That's badass."

"Hopefully my kid will be proud of me."

"Of course it will. Do you want a boy or a girl?"

"Doesn't matter."

Dahlia asks me a thousand and one questions about babies and pregnancy and my plans until I forget that my heart is in pieces and that I can't have the one man I've fallen in love with.

She talks me down until my eyelids are heavy and I finally fall asleep.

TWO DAYS LATER, I have dinner at Frank and Tina's and I tell them about the pregnancy.

"Who... Who is the father?" Frank asks as he clears his throat. He doesn't make eye contact and I know he's supremely uncomfortable.

"You know who it is, Frank," I smile. The Prince and I have been having Sunday meals with the Valencias for months, now.

"It's Prince Charlie, isn't it?" Tina says, her hawk eyes drilling into mine. "I saw the way he was looking at you."

I blush and my lower lip trembles.

"And does the Prince know?" Tina asks.

I take a deep breath, ready to deny it again, but I know it's no use. My parents are staring at me, wide-eyed. I nod. "Yeah, he knows."

"What did he say?"

"He's engaged now, Tina. It's not... It won't work."

"Well, tell him to get un-engaged." Frank grunts. "Next time I see that man..."

"The King chose his fiancée. It's not as simple as it is for commoners." I try to sound more confident than I feel.

"Seems simple to me," Frank grunts. His cheeks have gone bright red and anger flashes in his eyes. "He's going to turn his back on you?"

"No! He wanted the baby." I take a deep breath. This is harder than I imagined. "It just wasn't meant to be."

Tina stares at me for a few long seconds, as if she's downloading my brain and analyzing it. Finally, she nods and reaches over to clasp my hand. "You want to keep this baby, don't you?"

"Yes," I say, a little more aggressively than I mean to. I put a hand protectively over my stomach.

Tina's lips twitch into a smile and she nods. "Good. We'll help you with anything you need. Won't we, Frank?"

"Of course. And next time that little prick of a Prince is at the shelter, I'll have a word with him." He starts mumbling to himself, shaking his head. "Knocking you up and leaving. I can't believe that. Does he have no sense of decency? What kind of guy—"

"It's okay, Frank," I interrupt. I smile sadly. "Please."

"You're on your own now, Elle," he says as he shakes his head. "It's tough to raise a kid on your own! He should know that. To walk away..."

"It's *okay*, Frank." Seeing how angry he is makes me feel a bit better. I walk over to the two of them and wrap my arms around them. "I love you. Thank you for being supportive."

"You're not on your own," Tina says. "You have us. Always."

Tina says all the right things, and Frank pretends that he isn't angry, and we sit down for a home-cooked meal together. Knowing that the Valencias are there for me eases my worries a little. After dinner, Tina takes me upstairs and into the attic. She pulls out an old box bursting with baby clothes.

"Tina, I didn't know you had all this stuff."

Sadness flashes over her face as she pinches her lips together. "We've had it for years. We tried, Frank and me. But it's like you said—it wasn't meant to be. But if we'd have had our own child, we wouldn't have started fostering kids, and we wouldn't have met you. You've brought so much joy into our life, Elle, I can't even put it into words. I'm so proud of you with all you've done at the university and with rowing... I wish you had more time for yourself before having this baby, but I know you'll be a wonderful mother."

She wraps me in a big hug and squeezes me tight. Tears sting my eyes and my throat is choked with emotion. I hug her back, soaking up all the love she has to give me.

Frank and Tina send me home with boxes of baby things. Tina promises to go to every doctor's appointment with me, and Frank helps me figure out a schedule with classes. It looks like I might be able to graduate a semester early if I take some classes during the summer, so I might get my degree before the baby comes. If I can figure out a way to pay for it, I might be able to graduate after all.

Between the Valencias and Dahlia, I'm starting to think that I can do this. But as I make my way back home, I glance at the castle in the distance and I wonder what Charlie is doing right now.

Is he thinking of me? Does he still want this baby? Will he forget about me?

Shaking my head, I turn my thoughts to my baby and my future. I can't have Charlie, and thinking of him only makes my heart ache.

What happened between us was wonderful, but it's over.

33

CHARLIE

OLIVIA BRUNDLE IS the most vapid woman I've ever met, and the thought of spending the rest of my life with her sends me into a deep, dark hole. I try to call Elle every day for a week, and I send her an embarrassing number of texts, but she doesn't answer any of them.

It's for the best—probably.

Or at least, that's what I tell myself.

I know she's right—we can't be together. My father won, and I have to marry some airhead and play by the rules so that he can keep pulling the Kingdom's strings.

It may be true, but it doesn't change the fact that I don't want to accept it. I just can't wrap my head around the fact that there's a woman who is perfect for me in every way, but I can't have her because she doesn't have some special last name.

It's bullshit.

But my mother's words ring in my head, and I know I have to do it. She once warned me that I would have to sacrifice things for the sake of duty. She told me that as the eldest, it would be my responsibility. Maybe she was in love once, and she had to give it up for the sake of the Kingdom.

With Damon in medical school, and Gabe a worse troublemaker than I ever was, I know I have to do this. My mother was right—I'm the only one with the strength and the will to be King.

Even so, all I want to do with the Crown is fling it deep into Farcliff Lake.

I spend another week wallowing in my own misery. I drive by Elle's house every day until it becomes too hard to go near her. I set aside some money for her and the baby, hiding it in an account my father can't access. I plan to pay her student fees for next year.

I torture myself, thinking of every single possibility where I could be with Elle, and not Olivia.

But there's no way. I have to accept the Crown, or else put Elle in danger of retribution and force one of my brothers to give up their lives. My father has me over a barrel, and I can't see any way out of it. If I don't do as he says, he'll renounce me as his heir and everyone that I love will suffer.

The entire Kingdom will suffer.

Whenever I go near his office, he shuts the door. I hear rumblings about this dam project, and it worries me. I still can't work out what's going on, but my head is a mess. I can't focus.

Two weeks after Elle tells me it's over between us, Olivia and her family are invited over to a formal dinner at the castle. I straighten my tie in the mirror as Neville waits by my bedroom door.

"How are you feeling, sir?"

"How am I feeling?" I scoff. "I'm feeling like shit. I have to marry a woman I have no interest in marrying, and the woman that I'm in love with is pretending she doesn't know me."

"I'm sorry, sir."

"Me, too." I walk to the ensuite to put some pomade in my hair. When I tug open the top drawer, a little black ring box slides to the front. Cracks spider over my heart for the millionth time. I flip the ring box open to see my mother's ring, and I know I'll never be able to give it to Elle.

Which means I'll never give it to anyone.

If Elle won't wear it, it'll stay hidden in this drawer forever.

With a sigh, I toss it back and slam the drawer shut. I fix my hair and stomp out. "Let's get this over with, Nev."

He bows and walks with me to the dining room. Everyone is already there: Damon, Gabe, my father, as well as Olivia and her parents.

It's a happy fucking family reunion.

"Glad you could join us," my father says with a cruel smile. For the past two weeks, he's been walking around with the same stupid smirk on his face. "Charles, you remember Lord and Lady Brundle?"

"Good to see you again," I say mechanically, even though I have no recollection of ever meeting them.

"Your father and I were just discussing the hydroelectric dam proposition on the southern end of Farcliff Lake."

I arch an eyebrow. Lord Brundle seems to be up to speed on this proposal. The dam would straddle our two countries, and I'm starting to wonder what my father promised him. Is Olivia being traded like a bargaining chip as well?

"Enough business, Daddy." Olivia bats her eyelashes at me. "Come sit, future husband." She gives me a toothy smile and pats the chair beside her.

I hold back a shiver of disgust. When I sit next to her, she puts her hand on my thigh. I move it off, and then throw a glassful of wine down my gullet and call for another. If I can't change this, at least I can drink, right? I haven't had a big binge in months.

Somewhere between my second and third glasses of alcohol, her hand reappears on my thigh. It slides all the way up until she's grabbing my...

"What the fuck?" I jump back, kicking the table and smacking her off me.

Cutlery clatters as Olivia's face reddens. She removes her hand and I glare at her.

"Charlie!" My father snaps. "That's no way to speak to your betrothed."

I don't answer, instead swinging my eyes to my future father-in-law. "Tell me more about this dam," I say to Lord Brundle.

My father's eyes narrow as Lord Brundle launches into an explanation of the new hydroelectric dam. Grimdale residents would be relocated to East Brundle while the current lowlands would be completely flooded.

"We estimate that the power generated would be enough to support both our countries."

"You want to relocate over twelve million people? How do you expect to do that? What would they do?"

"It's just Grimdale," my father says with a wave. "They'll move."

"*Just* Grimdale? They're people, Father. They're *your* subjects. You'll just move them to a different country without batting an eyelid? What will they do in Brundle?"

My father just smiles at me, and dread seeps into my heart. This isn't just about Elle, or my brothers. If I refuse to marry Olivia, he'll be in power long enough to see this plan through. If I do marry her, I'm essentially signing on the dotted line to hand over all of Grimdale to Brundle. He's getting rid of what he sees as the scourge of our Kingdom—the entirety Grimdale—and making a shitload of money for himself in the process.

At the same time, he's getting rid of the only threat he has—me.

Check-fucking-mate.

All those people moved from their homes in Grimdale... for what? How much money is this power plant going to generate?

"We have a shortage of workers in East Brundle. Lots of jobs."

"What kind of jobs?" My eyes narrow.

Lord Brundle waves a hand. "Factories, mines, that sort of thing. Low-skilled jobs well-suited to Grimdale residents."

"You do realize that people have been living in Grimdale for generations, right? They're not just animals that you can trade for money. They're not all low-skilled workers. There are doctors and lawyers and all kinds of professionals in Grimdale, too. They won't move without a fight."

"Well, that'll be something for the new King to deal with," my father says, raising a glass. "To the happy couple."

"To the happy couple," Lady Brundle says with a smile.

My heart sinks. My father is triumphant. If I oppose this now, he'll hurt Elle. If I don't, I'm the face of the project. My father keeps calling the shots with no repercussions.

I know, now, that Elle is right. I can't be with her. My duty is to my Kingdom, and it seems that my father is intent on ruining it. If I turn my back on the Crown now, all of Grimdale will be annihilated.

My father stares at me with a wicked smirk on his face. He calls for more wine, but I can't hear a word. My ears are ringing. I look around the dinner table to see my brothers' grim faces followed by my father's jubilant one.

He knows he's trapped me. The only way I can stop this from happening is by becoming King, and the only way I can become King is by marrying Olivia Brundle.

Which means I can't have Elle.

Sitting at that dinner table, the last piece of my heart turns black and crumbles as I realize that for all my wishing, all my hopes and late-night dreams... I'll never be with the woman I love. I'll never be a father to our child. I'll never hold her in my arms again and I'll never get to tell her that I love her.

I have to choose between her and half my Kingdom. As much as it breaks my spirit, I have to choose my Kingdom.

34

ELLE

DAYS TURN INTO WEEKS, which turn into months. My baby grows. I take summer classes and schedule my next semester so I can graduate by December.

The baby is due around the holidays, so it'll be tough, but it's possible. I just have to do things right.

I apply for student loans. Between that, what the Valencias scrape together, and a generous loan from Dahlia, I'm able to pay tuition for the summer and fall semesters. I'll graduate.

I stay off social media and I don't watch the news. Stories of Prince Charlie's wedding dominate the press. It's never-ending.

There are news stories about what flowers will be chosen, what dress Olivia will wear, what they'll name their first child. It feels like whenever I'm having a good day, I'll see another headline about his happy marriage, or a photo of him and Olivia together, and it sends me down another spiral of depression.

The only thing that keeps me going is my baby. When I feel the negativity start to creep in, I sit and meditate until it goes away. I play classical music for my bump, and talk to my baby as if it's already in my arms.

"You're going to be the luckiest baby in the world, because you have a mother who will do anything for you," I whisper to my belly.

Tina brings me to my doctor's appointments, and I learn that I'm having a son.

"What are you going to call him?" She asks as she's driving me home.

"Charlie," I answer, staring out the window. She reaches over to clasp my hand, and we drive the rest of the way home in silence.

I still love him, is the thing. Even when I read about Prince Charlie's upcoming marriage. Even when I see pictures of him with the girl who tormented me in the locker room for three years. Even when I get scared that I won't be able to provide for this baby on my own.

I still love him.

As the weeks go by, I realize it'll never go away.

So, I just accept it. I'll love the Prince from afar, and I'll use that energy to raise our son.

COME SEPTEMBER, I go to the Farcliff University Student Services building to make my final tuition payment, only to learn that the balance has been cleared.

I walk out, stroking my now-obvious six-month baby bump. I know it was him—it was the Prince. My fingers hover over my phone screen, but I hesitate. I've blocked his number months ago, because I couldn't handle his calls and texts.

If I talk to him now, will I still have the strength to go on without him? I'm just starting to come to terms with his absence.

I put my phone away without saying anything and I go home. Dahlia is there, and I try to give her back the money she lent me. Dahlia refuses, saying I'll need money to live during the semester.

"I won't charge you interest. The banks will. Pay back the student loans first, and you can pay me back after."

"Dahlia…"

"I'm not taking any money from you. I'll kick you out of this house before that happens, and then you'll need the money even more than you do now."

I open my mouth, but all I can do is laugh. "Fine. Thank you." And then my jaw drops and my hand goes to my stomach. "He's kicking!"

Dahlia squeals, rushing over to me and putting her hand out to feel it. "Is this the first time?"

I nod, speechless. My cheeks flush and a smile cracks my face in half. "That feels so weird."

"You have an actual whole other human growing inside you," Dahlia says, her eyes wide. "That's wild."

I laugh. "Yes, that's the general idea behind pregnancy."

We sit on the sofa together for another quiet evening, and I realize that Dahlia and the Valencias are all the family I need. I've spent my whole life mourning the fact that I don't know who my parents are, but now—with this baby inside me—it's giving me perspective. I get to choose my family, and fill it with people who love and care about me. I know Dahlia, Frank, and Tina will be here for me, no matter what.

I glance at Dahlia and nod to her room. "I haven't heard any marathon sex sessions in a while. You okay?"

She gives me a tight smile. "Yeah," she says. "Just a dry spell, I guess. Don't want to ruin another bed frame seeing as you won't be able to help me build another one for a little while."

I laugh, and then glance at my friend. It's out of character for her to be celibate. "You okay?"

"I'm fine. You?"

"Yeah," I smile. "I'm good, actually. I feel... I feel like everything is going to be okay."

"Didn't I tell you that four months ago? It *will* be okay."

She grabs the remote and changes the channel, and Charlie's face flashes on the screen. My heart squeezes.

"Oops! Sorry," she says, flicking it back.

"Wait, go back."

"*...and the date of the wedding is set for November first of this year. With only six weeks for the final preparations, the castle is abuzz with energy. The Brundle family are making preparations to move their daughter to Farcliff...*"

"Six weeks," I say, eyebrows arching. "That's soon."

"Must be some kind of rush."

"Maybe she's pregnant, too," I say with a grin that turns into a grimace. As soon as the words leave my mouth, I regret saying them out loud. My lips pinch and my eyes water, and Dahlia squeezes my arm.

"I don't think so," she says. "I don't think he would do that."

"Yeah," I respond, but I don't really believe her. The Prince and I aren't together anymore. He's getting married, and he's expected to have to have children—legitimate children—to become his heirs. At some point, if it hasn't happened already, he's going to have sex with Olivia Brundle.

The thought of him with another woman still makes me sick. My stomach turns and the baby kicks, as if he can feel me getting upset. I just run my hands over my stomach and focus on my son. I take deep breaths as Dahlia changes the channel again, and I push the thought of the Prince and Olivia out of my mind.

It doesn't matter anymore, but it still hurts.

"He loved you, Elle. I know he did." Dahlia's voice is soft.

"It's irrelevant," I say. "It's over. I just need to move on."

"I'm sorry, Elle."

"For what? I mean, at the end of the day, I was with him and it gave me an entire new perspective on life. I'll have this kid, now, and I already know I'll love him more than anything else in the world. It's not all bad."

"No, but it would be better if he wasn't on television every four seconds."

I laugh bitterly. "Yeah, true. I'll have to choose a less famous secret boyfriend next time."

"He hasn't tried to contact you?"

"I blocked his number."

"Oh."

"He was calling me almost every day the first month. It was too hard to keep ignoring his calls. I can't be with him, so it's easier just to cut him off."

"He paid your tuition, though, right?"

"Yeah."

"So he's thinking about you."

"Maybe."

Dahlia doesn't say much after that, and neither do I.

Maybe I should talk to him and keep him in my life. Maybe I should call him to thank him. It would be the mature thing to do.

But every time I see him with Olivia, my heart breaks all over again. I'm scared that if I talk to him, hearing his voice will send me back down to the depths of despair.

It's easier just to move on. It happened, and it was great, but now it's done. I'll always love him, but I can never have him. It's over.

35

CHARLIE

MY WEDDING DAY feels more like a funeral. With my stiff, over-starched ceremonial uniform choking me, and my hair gelled back like a helmet, I feel like a fool. A makeup artist is fussing over my face and neck. She's covered my visible tattoos with makeup on my chest and wrists—at my father's instruction, of course. It's not appropriate, he told her. I don't have the energy to fight it. It's just another sign that I can't be who I want to be anymore.

"It's okay. I'm done now," I say, waving her away.

"But the photos—"

"The photos will be fine. I don't care about the photos." I get up off the chair and make my way down to the castle lobby. The royal procession is ready and waiting for me. We'll make our way to the cathedral in the center of Farcliff. The police have closed off the streets, and there are already thousands of people lining the barricades to watch us go by.

My carriage is ornate, red, and completely over-the-top. Four white horses are ready to pull me to the end of my life as I know it.

My father hangs out of the carriage waiting behind mine and he waves impatiently. "You're late!"

I ignore him. Castle guards on horses line the procession on either side, wearing equally ridiculous uniforms as me. What a fucking rigamarole this is. It's almost embarrassing.

Olivia Brundle is somewhere in this circus, wearing a big dress that everyone will gush about. There are about a dozen horse-drawn carriages in a row, and I allow myself to be led to one of them. Neville joins me, along with my two brothers.

"You look like you're in a good mood," Gabe says with a grin. "Your wedding day is supposed to be happy."

"Yeah, well, it's not."

No one says anything else, and we start moving. The carriage bounces along and I stare out the window, seeing nothing.

The future is bleak, but this is what being King is all about, apparently. I have to sacrifice my personal happiness for the sake of my people—and the twelve million residents of Grimdale shouldn't have to move away from their homes. If I can't be with Elle, I'll make sure of that, at least.

The Farcliff Dam Project isn't signed yet, and I'm making it my mission to kill it, if it's the last thing I do. I don't know how I'll do it, but I will. I'm doing it for Elle, and for my mother. It's what they'd both want.

There are thousands of people lining the streets, shouting and cheering for us as we ride by. My spirits sink lower. They shouldn't be here celebrating when I feel like I'm walking the plank. We wind through the streets of Farcliff and the crowds get denser.

As we near the cathedral, the energy outside grows more frantic. People jostle and push to be near the barricades, throwing their arms toward the royal carriages. Cameras flash. People shout.

Our procession comes to a stop outside the cathedral. Damon shakes my hand and exits the carriage. Gabe is next. I watch them take their places outside the carriage and I turn to Neville, who's holding something in his hands.

"Your Highness..."

It's my mother's ring box.

"Put that away, Neville. Olivia Brundle isn't wearing that ring. Never."

"I think you should look inside." He stares at me and thrusts the box toward me.

I huff. I don't want to look at that ring right now. That ring represents everything that I'm giving up, everything that I've lost. But Neville nods at me, and it's uncharacteristic for him to be this pushy. I open the box, and my mother's emerald ring twinkles at me.

My chest squeezes and I struggle to take a breath.

"What? Why am I looking at this?"

Nev clears his throat. "Look underneath."

I frown, pulling up the cushion that holds the ring. A small, folded slip of paper is hidden underneath. My mouth goes dry. I stare at Neville, who averts his eyes.

"Did you know this was in here?"

"The Queen was very clear that you should only find it on your own. But, seeing as the circumstances are what they are..."

I unfold the yellowing paper with trembling hands. My breath hitches when I see my mother's looping handwriting. In the center of the page is a little circular watermark, where the ink has bled, as if she cried as she wrote this.

My darling Charlie,

If you're reading this, it means my worst fears have been realized. I'm sorry that I'm not there to see your wedding day, or my grandchildren, or to see what kind of man you grew to be.

I want you to know that I love you with all my heart, and I'm so very proud of you. You will be the King that Farcliff needs.

My hands are shaking so hard I can't read. My vision is blurring. I take a breath to compose myself.

In the cabin, at the back of the wine cellar, you'll find a safe. The combination is your birthday. I've hidden evidence of the first attempt on my life, and everything that I believe shows that your father and Talin Thorne are planning to have me murdered.

I'm causing too much of a fuss with Farcliff politics, I think. You know me—always sticking my nose in where it doesn't belong. Kind of like you.

Take care of your brothers.

Love,
Mom

I read the letter again, my eyes widening.

"Sir?" Neville asks. "What does it say?"

"It says she thought she was going to be murdered," I whisper. "It says my father and Talin... Thorne?" My eyes widen. "I thought his last name was Smith."

Neville's eyebrows arch. "I always heard Smith. Thorne was..."

"The name of my governess."

My hands tremble as my pulse quickens. I smooth the paper out and snap a picture of it with my phone. It takes me three tries to get a picture that isn't blurry because my hands are shaking so much. I fold the letter up again, putting it into the ring box and slipping the box into my jacket pocket. I pat it to make sure it's safe as my eyes swing to look out of the carriage window. My brothers are walking up the cathedral steps. Talin is standing near the door, hands clasped behind his back, and the urge to murder him becomes almost irresistible.

Cameras flash.

My blood boils.

Tabitha Raventhal was right. My mother was murdered, and I know who did it.

Flying out the door before anyone can open it for me, I stumble toward my father's carriage at the back of the procession. People clamor for my attention, but I ignore them all.

Tearing the King's carriage door off its hinges, I glare at my father. "You set me up."

"Get in that cathedral and marry the Brundle girl."

"You killed my mother."

"Been talking to the Raventhals, have you?"

"No, I've got a letter from my mother—the Queen that you had murdered—that explains it all." It's not quite true, I don't know everything, but I know enough. "And Talin... I know his last name is Thorne. I know he's related to the governess, and you were behind it all. You set me up to be preyed on by a grown woman. You had me abused. You had my mother killed."

My whole body is shaking and my father crouches away from me, eyes wide. He shakes his head. "You have no proof."

"I have enough. You think the Kingdom will care that I'm in love with Elle when they hear that you murdered your own wife? That you had your own child set up by a grown woman? That you threatened him? I don't need you to name me heir, because you're going to abdicate. Today."

"I will do no such—"

"I have pictures of the letter, and I'll send them to every news station I can find. You're going to jail."

"No one will believe you."

"They will when I tell them about the dam project. How do you think the twelve million residents of Grimdale will react when they hear you killed the one member of the royal family who cared about them and are planning to flood their homes?" I lean in toward him. "They'll tear you limb from limb, Father, and I'll let them. They'll put your head on a stake, and I'll laugh with them."

"Charlie..." My father opens and closes his mouth, running his hands through his hair. His whole face has gone red and he sputters and tries to speak, but nothing comes out.

"I'm not getting married today. You're getting up there and abdicating."

His lip trembles and he closes his eyes, but he still shakes his head. "I will not—"

"Either step down right now, or watch everything you built crumble. If you step down, I'll keep this quiet. If you make a fuss, you'll welcome the day that you die."

For once, the cruel grin is on my lips, not his. He knows that he'll be dishonored, dethroned, destroyed if a word of this gets out.

I won't even need all the proof in my hands. My mother's letter is enough. A whiff of suspicion is enough.

And after everything he's put me through over the past seven months, I'll enjoy every second of his fall. The King won't be building that dam, he won't be pulling the strings in this Kingdom, and most importantly—he won't be forcing me to marry Olivia fucking Brundle.

The King just stares at me, defeated, and I walk away.

I turn to one of the guards flanking our procession. "Get off the horse," I say, nodding to the tall white mount.

"Sir?"

"I said get off the fucking horse."

The guard frowns at me, but he obeys.

I wish I could say riding a horse is like riding a bike—but I'm out of practice, and it shows. I swing my leg over the saddle and almost go tumbling over the other side as I lose my balance. The horse moves nervously underneath me as I settle into the saddle. I pat its neck and make soft noises until the beast settles.

"What's this horse's name?" I ask the guard.

"Karma, Your Highness."

I grin. "Perfect." I lean down over Karma's neck. "You're going to take me to Elle, okay, Karma?"

The massive white gelding snorts in response. I grin.

"Charlie! You can't cancel the wedding now." My father appears in the carriage window, hanging out of it. His face is twisted in anger.

"I can do whatever the fuck I want. You've got nothing over me. I'm not marrying the Brundle girl, and I'm not building that dam."

The King just stares at me and then swears loudly and disappears inside the carriage again. I turn the horse around and start trotting down the street.

Reporters shout at me from the other side of the barriers. A police barricade blocks the way toward Elle's house, and I lean down to my horse's ear.

"I need you to trust me on this one, okay?" I pat his neck and grip the reins as I take a deep breath. "We're getting out of here, and we're finding my woman."

The horse snorts again. I kick my heels in and we take off toward the barricade. We start at a slow trot, and I squeeze my legs against Karma again. My heart thumps as the barricade approaches. I haven't ridden a horse since I was a kid, but instinct takes over.

Karma speeds up, and I urge him faster and faster. The barricade comes rushing at us, and my heart is in my throat. It looms closer as people scream around us. When we're only a few feet away from it, I think I've made a mistake.

A terrible, terrible mistake.

We're going to crash into it. I'm going to break my neck.

But Karma knows what to do. He launches himself into the air and we clear the barricade effortlessly. Well, Karma clears it effortlessly—I cling on for dear life. We land on the other side, and I pull the reins up to slow him down, gulping down panicked breaths as my heart tries to run away from me. Karma is excited. The horse rears up on its hind legs, kicking and neighing as I do my best to stay in the saddle.

I grip Karma with everything I've got, praying that I don't fall on my ass. With my horses on its hind legs, I smile at the flashing cameras.

Put this on the front of your stupid newspapers.

"Come on, Karma. Take me to my love. *Hiyah!*"

We take off at a hard gallop down the streets. Karma doesn't hesitate. He's fast and powerful, and he doesn't break stride even once.

This is better than a motorcycle. It's more exhilarating than anything I've ever done. I can hear cars starting behind me, and I know I'm being followed.

I don't care. Let them follow. Let them see what their new King really cares about.

We gallop down the streets, jumping another barricade and bringing traffic to a standstill. A crowd forms behind me, following as best they can as I make my way toward the little bungalow on the edge of Grimdale that I've come to love.

To Elle.

To my love.

I ride Karma with a smile on my face, with my heart singing and my soul happy. There are a million things for me to find out, I have my father to deal with and Olivia to break up with... but none of that matters.

The only thing that matters is Elle.

My steed is covered in a thin coat of sweat by the time we get to Elle's house. I dismount and stumble, almost falling flat on my face before catching myself at the last moment. The front door flies open and a very pregnant, very beautiful Elle appears in the doorway.

She steals my breath away. I haven't seen her in months, and my heart almost explodes from happiness.

"What in the...?" She has one hand on her stomach and the other on her forehead. "What are you doing here?"

I falter as I walk toward her, Karma panting behind me.

"Elle," I say, falling to my knees. "Marry me."

36

ELLE

I THINK I'm having another weird pregnancy dream.

The Crown Prince of Farcliff just galloped into my front yard on a massive white horse, fell to his knees and proposed.

Bringing my hand to the opposite underarm, I pinch my skin—*hard*. It has to be a dream. There's no other explanation.

But pain shoots through my skin and I don't wake up.

The Prince is panting. His horse whinnies and snorts behind him, and then wanders up and nuzzles Charlie's ear. Charlie's still staring up at me, arms outstretched.

"Well? What do you say, Elle... make me the happiest man in Farcliff."

"I... I thought you were marrying another woman."

"No, I'm not. Not anymore."

"What about your brothers? The Kingdom? Your duty?"

"I found a way, Elle. It's all going to be okay." He stands up and cups my face in his hands. "Stop torturing me and tell me you'll be my wife. Please. It's killing me. I don't want anyone else, I only want you. These past seven months have been the worst months of my life, Elle. I can't live without you."

"What about the King? What about the throne?"

"Elle," he says, laughing almost maniacally. "Listen to me. It's over. It's fine. The throne is mine... and yours, if you'll have me."

"This isn't a joke?"

Tears are streaming down both our faces and he shakes his head. My whole body trembles as I try to make sense of what's happening. He brings his forehead to mine and holds me.

"This is the furthest thing from a joke. I love you more than anyone or anything else in the world. I can't imagine my life without you and our child at my side. I want you to rule Farcliff with me, to be the mother of my children and the Queen of this Kingdom. Marry me, please. Don't make me beg."

His words finally start to sink in. I hear the thumping of feet and honking of horns in the distance, but all I can see is Charlie.

My lips tug at the corners. "I don't know, I kind of like it when you beg."

Charlie's chest heaves up and down as he gulps down another breath. I run my fingers over his cheek. He sighs, closing his eyes and leaning into my touch.

"What about Olivia?" I ask in a whisper.

"I never wanted her. Never touched her. My father just wanted me to marry her for political reasons, but it doesn't matter anymore. Elle, you're not listening to me. Nothing matters except you."

"You're serious?" My voice cracks, and I run my fingers into his hair.

"Deadly serious."

"You really want to marry me?"

"With every fiber of my soul."

My heart thumps. My cheeks are soaked. I bite my lip and take a deep breath. "For real?"

His face splits into a laugh and the Prince lifts me up over his head, spinning me in a slow circle. "Yes, Elle. Yes!"

Vaguely, at the back of my mind, I see flashes from a dozen cameras and I hear voices and shouts getting nearer.

It doesn't matter.

Charlie puts me back on my feet and crushes his lips to mine. His hand drifts over my stomach and his lips tangle with mine. With one hand cupping my cheek, and the other on my stomach, Charlie leans his forehead against mine and sighs.

Happiness bubbles up inside me and I can't hold back my laughter. I smile, I laugh, I cry. I intertwine my fingers with his on my stomach and lean into him as my heart explodes.

Charlie kisses me again and again, holding me close as if he's afraid of letting me go. Dahlia appears at the door and starts swatting reporters back so that we have a bit of space on the front stoop of my run-down Grimdale home.

Then, the Prince gets down on one knee and reaches into his suit jacket. He pulls out a little black velvet box and flips it open.

I gasp.

I've seen that ring before—everyone in the Kingdom has. The green emerald stone belonged to the Queen of Farcliff, Charlie's mother. It was thought to be lost when she died. But it's right here, in front of me, and Charlie wants me to have it.

Me!

"Elle, be my wife."

"Ask me nicely," I say through my tears as my face splits into a smile.

Charlie laughs. "Elle, light of my life, mother of my child, and the key to my heart and happiness, will you please, for the love of Farcliff, *please* marry me?"

I'm still laughing and crying, and Dahlia is still swatting reporters back. She glances back at me.

"Say 'yes' now, Elle. Christ, woman! Put him out of his misery!"

I can't speak, because I have no voice. I just nod as tears stream down my face. "Yes," I croak. "I'll marry you."

When he slides the ring on my hand, the Prince lets out a sigh. My cheeks hurt from smiling so much. I wrap my arms around him and he kisses me again.

My love, my King, my future husband.

When we turn to the cameras, I'm beaming. I can't help it. I know there will be questions to be answered—this doesn't make sense to me yet. It probably doesn't make sense to anyone except Charlie.

But I do know that it feels right.

The Prince's butler, Neville, appears in a black car and Dahlia helps us make it through the crowd to get to the vehicle. Neville drives us down the road in silence, and I lean my forehead against Charlie's shoulder.

I take a deep breath. "This is real, right? It's not a dream. I don't think I'd survive if I have to wake up from this."

"It's not a dream," Charlie assures me.

I sigh, squeezing his hand with mine. We lose the reporters behind us, and Neville drives us up to our own little place, nestled deep in the forests of Farcliff. We drive up to the cabin at the southern end of the lake, and I take a deep breath.

Neville nods to us and drives away. Charlie leads me to the door. "Welcome home, my Queen."

I grin. "I like the sound of that."

"So do I."

In that cabin in the woods, Charlie wraps me in his arms and kisses me tenderly. We laugh, and cry, and kiss. He tells me everything that's happened and for a few blissful hours, we forget about the rest of the world. There will be a mess to deal with, but for now... it's just us.

Dahlia was right, after all. Everything worked out just fine.

EPILOGUE
ELLE

THAT DAY, we found the evidence that Charlie's mother had gathered and hidden in the cabin's wine cellar. It turns out that an attempt had been made on her life once before, during a ski trip a year before her death. She'd managed to trace the assassin and even connected him to the Thornes, but wasn't able to go public before she was murdered.

We had photos, names, dates—leaving a very clear picture of who was behind it. Combined with the letter she wrote and the news of the Farcliff Dam Project, it was enough to get the King to step down. Talin Thorne was imprisoned.

I kept pushing for Charlie to arrest his father, too, but he never did. I think after his scandal with the governess, the last thing he wanted to do was cause controversy at the very beginning of his rule.

Instead, the King abdicated and moved away from Farcliff. Charlie, Damon, and Gabriel mourned the death of their mother and invited the Raventhals back to the castle.

Damon, especially, took it hard.

It was a tough time. In a way, the Princes lost their mother all over again, and lost their father at the same time. Charlie was very serious and quiet during those days.

WE WERE MARRIED IN A QUIET, closed ceremony. Charlie dug out my one pair of heels from the bottom drawer of his dresser, but I was too pregnant to wear them to the wedding. We had them framed instead.

I gave birth three days later to a healthy baby boy, and Charlie doted on his son all day, every day. Having a baby in the castle brightened everyone's mood and distracted them from the tragedy of the Queen's death and the sudden abdication of the King.

The love that Charlie and I had for one another, and for our baby, won over the people. They accepted me as their Queen more easily than I ever expected, and Charlie and I started ruling with the full support of both Farcliff and Grimdale.

I graduated from Farcliff University, but I didn't have to worry about providing for the baby. I asked Dahlia to be the baby's godmother, and she gleefully accepted—she had her own reasons for wanting to be at the castle, after all.

The Valencias refused to move to the castle with the Prince and me. Frank said he wouldn't be able to run the shelter from Farcliff Castle. They did accept funding for the mobile spay and neuter units, though, and Frank became the face of animal shelters in Farcliff.

A year and a half after Charlie Jr. was born, I crawled into bed beside Charlie with a smile plastered over my face.

"What?" He asked, grinning.

I took his hand and placed it over my stomach. I stared at him, happiness overflowing in my heart.

"You're..."

I nodded. "I'm pregnant. You ready to be a dad again?"

Charlie's smile widened, and he crushed his lips against mine. He laughed and kissed me over and over, and my poor heart nearly exploded. I didn't know it was possible to be that happy.

Now, ten years later, we have three wonderful children and my life is so full of love that I can hardly believe it. Dahlia is like a sister to me in more ways than one... but that's her story, and I'll let her tell it in her own words.

Charlie is beloved by the entire Kingdom of Farcliff, and he's proven himself over and over to be a kind and just King. His mother's memory lives on in him.

I don't know what I've done to deserve this much love and happiness, but I'm grateful for it every day. My three children are tall, strong, and athletic, and I make sure they know that they're beautiful just as they are.

In the evenings, Charlie wraps his arms around me and tells me he loves me. Even after a decade, I never tire of hearing it.

"My Queen," he says, running his hands over my body. "Have I ever told you how wonderful you are?"

"Every day," I smile, closing my eyes and enjoying his touch.

"I love you, Elle," King Charlie sighs into my ear.

My heart flutters, just as it did the very first day. "I love you, too." I kiss him tenderly, and he pulls me close.

Just like the very first night we had together, heat sparks between my thighs. I fall into his arms, and he claims me as his Queen.

The only difference is that now, I know we aren't doomed. There's no expiration date, no end, no fall from a great height. We have each other, forever—happily ever after.

EXTENDED EPILOGUE

1

ELLE

My feet hurt, my back is sore, and I'm so tired I can't walk straight... but I'm happy.

No, I'm more than happy. I'm complete. I'm so full of joy that it feels like my heart can't possibly hold it all.

Charlie leads me away from the Great Hall and up to his —well, *our*—bed chambers. My wedding dress is sticking to me and the sweat gathers between my shoulder blades. My heart soars and my cheeks hurt from smiling so much.

His arm is strong and supportive around my shoulders.

I lean into him with a sigh. "The wedding was perfect. Thank you for making it private."

"Of course," Charlie answers. "That's what I wanted, too. After everything that happened with my father, I didn't want to have a camera stuck in my face all night. I just wanted to celebrate us—the way it's always been. You and me, and the people that mean something to us."

"We can release some photos to the press tomorrow— keep them happy." I smile at him. "I know the press have already asked you for more information."

"The people want to see their new Queen."

My heart flutters and a smile drifts over my face. "That's a sentence I never thought I'd hear."

"You're going to hear it a lot more times in your life." Charlie looks at me as his eyes shine. "I love you."

We walk arm in arm to our bedroom, kick off our shoes, and collapse into bed. I'm so tired that I don't think I can even manage to take my dress off. Charlie's shirt is open, but he's still fully clothed, too. My belly looks huge as I stare down at it, running my hands over the bump.

Charlie reaches over and intertwines his fingers with mine. "Not too long, now."

"He's due in two weeks."

His hand squeezes mine and I lean into him. The baby kicks, as if responding to us. Charlie chuckles, pressing his lips to my abdomen.

"He's going to be good at sports, I can tell."

"Well, with a mother like me..." I try to laugh, but it comes out as a croak. I'm too tired. My eyelids are already heavy, and the weight of Charlie's body in bed next to me is making me sleepy.

I feel him move around, and he helps to take my dress off. I fall asleep not long afterward.

I WAKE up with Charlie's leg thrown over mine, and his arm across my chest. The baby is kicking. The weak winter sunlight is streaming through the window, and I can tell it's going to be a cold day outside.

But when I glance down at my finger where my wedding band glimmers, the cold doesn't matter. Nothing matters, because I have everything I could possibly want, right here in bed with me.

Charlie stirs beside me and lets out a sigh. "I slept so well," he groans. "I don't want to get up yet."

"So don't," I chuckle. I nuzzle into his shoulder. We lay there for a while, drifting somewhere between wakefulness and sleep.

"Did you see Damon and Dahlia?" Charlie asks after a time. His hand is running up and down my spine, lulling me into a peaceful sort of daze.

"What do you mean?"

"They were giving each other the eye last night," Charlie says. "They disappeared together at one point."

My eyes spring open and I push myself up to lean on my elbow. "They did?"

"You didn't notice?"

"No! When was this?"

"Right before dinner started."

"I can't believe I missed that. Do you think..."

Charlie grins. "I don't know. I've never seen Damon with a girlfriend, but then again, I've never seen him look at anyone the way he looked at her."

"Can you imagine? Oh, that would be perfect!"

Charlie's smile slips the tiniest bit, and I wonder what he's thinking about. Maybe Damon has a dark side I don't know about—or maybe he's worried that Dahlia might not be welcome by the people of Farcliff, considering her past. Maybe he's thinking of his own mother, and Tabitha Raventhal's relationship to her.

I lay back down on his chest and shake the thought away. Maybe the two of them just went for a quiet walk together. Maybe they hooked up, and it was a one-time thing. Just because I got married yesterday doesn't mean that everyone else is in love, too.

"Damon likes her," Charlie says, reading my thoughts.

"He likes Dahlia?"

He grunts in agreement. "I could tell way back when she came to the castle for dinner. You know, when I was trying to pretend like I didn't know you?"

"Oh, how times have changed," I laugh. "Look at you now."

"Now, I can't get enough of you," he grows. He kisses me, and then kisses my baby bump, and we laze in bed for another hour more.

2

CHARLIE

"Push!" The nurse is coaching Elle through labor, and I'm trying my best to be supportive.

Elle is red-faced and sweaty, blowing air out of her mouth as her eyes focus on something on the far wall. People are talking, the doctor is saying something, Elle is grunting.

I'm standing beside her, trying not to wince as she crushes my hand in her vice-like grip. Pain shoots up my arm but I grit my teeth and stand there, trying to be as supportive as I can.

It's a blur.

Elle grunts, moans through her teeth, and finally lets out a roaring scream. My eyes water as she crushes my hand a bit harder.

"That's it," the doctor says, nodding in encouragement. "Almost there."

I can't focus on anything. Elle is in pain, I'm in pain, and in mere seconds, I'm going to be a father. I can't breathe. My knees start to quake.

The baby is right on time—wanting to come out exactly

on his due date of December 4th, two weeks after our wedding.

The wedding seems like a distant memory now.

Everything seems like a distant memory. The edges of my vision are starting to go black, with dots clouding in toward the center of my eyes as I try to focus on staying vertical.

"Stop pushing now," the nurse says, and Elle's grip on my hand relaxes a bit. My vision clears, and I take the first full breath I've managed in a few minutes. Elle inhales shakily, and I brush hair off her brow. I lean over to press my lips against her forehead before grunting.

"Sweaty," I hear myself saying as I wipe my mouth on the back of my hand.

Elle swings her eyes to mine, and my blood turns to ice. Never in my life have I ever seen Elle look at me with such venom. Her lips twitch into a snarl but before she can say anything, it's time for her to push again.

I think the bones in my hand snap, she grips them so hard.

I fold at the waist, catching myself on the bed as pain shoots through my arm. It's nothing compared to the pain she's feeling, I try to remember, but I can hardly breathe.

The seconds tick by, each of them lasting an eternity. I'm starting to panic. Is everything okay? Is this how it's supposed to happen?

Elle is in so much pain, it hurts me, too. Her face is redder than I've ever seen it, and she's making noises I didn't know she was able to make.

Everyone is talking at once.

My ears are ringing.

Once again, I feel unsteady and my vision is starting to fade. I don't have much time. I need for this to be over, or else

I need to get out of this fucking room—but at the same time, I can't leave Elle.

I suck a breath in through my teeth as I lose the feeling in the hand that Elle's crushing. Each breath takes effort.

And then, all of a sudden, it's over. Everyone relaxes.

My eyes widen, my vision clears, and I look down at the doctor, holding my son.

All I can see is blood. Blood covering the baby, blood between Elle's legs, blood on the hospital gown. They warned me there would be blood and amniotic fluid, but they didn't warn me that it would look like a fucking crime scene.

I think I'm going to throw up. Or pass out.

Or both.

"Would you like to cut the umbilical cord?" The doctor looks at me and a nurse presents me with a pair of sharp-looking shears... that they want me to use in close proximity to my newborn son?

No fucking way.

I still can't feel my hand, and I've lost my voice. I shake my head weakly, unable to utter a sound. Elle says something, but it sounds like she's underwater.

I'm definitely going to puke.

My knees knock together as the nurses and doctor work around us. I try to breathe in, but everything is becoming harder. My vision is darkening by the instant.

I stumble to the side.

Vaguely, I hear someone shout, "We have a fainter!"

And then everything goes dark.

WHEN I WAKE UP, I'm lying in a hospital bed in the hallway outside Elle's room. A nurse is standing next to me. She's and older woman with a no-nonsense demeanor.

"You didn't think to warn us that you were going to faint in there?" She tuts.

"I didn't know."

She shakes her head. "Everyone knows when they're about to faint. Come on, give me your arm, I'm taking your blood pressure."

"The baby—" I try to sit up.

"The baby is fine. Lie down."

I consider reminding her that I'm her King, but for some reason I think her response would be the same. She takes my blood pressure and jots down the numbers on a chart. Then, she looks at me with pursed lips.

"Can you sit up?"

I nod, lifting myself up. My head is ringing.

"Good," she says. "Sit there and don't move until I tell you to."

"My son—"

"You'll see your son in a minute, Your Majesty. Right now, I want to make sure you don't fall over and split your head open, okay?"

She stares me down until I nod, and I stay seated outside the door. A couple of seconds later, I hear the cries of an infant, followed by Elle's voice trying to soothe it.

My heart leaps into my throat.

I know what the nurse said, but I can't help it. I slip off the edge of the hospital bed and pause, making sure my legs still work.

When I make it to the doorway, Elle is holding our son in her arms, smiling and cooing down at him. She's still red in the face, sweaty, and her gown is covered in blood...

...and she's fucking gorgeous.

I shuffle into the room and find a chair next to her bed.

Her eyes are shining when she looks at me, and a smile stretches over her lips.

"Little Charlie," she whispers, turning her eyes back to our baby.

I've never felt anything like this. I reach over and touch my baby's skin for the first time, and my heart feels like it's exploding. Happiness, euphoria—and an absolute, gut-wrenching fear that I'm going to mess this up.

But the baby's fingers curl around my thumb, and my heart flips again.

"How are you feeling?" Elle asks, fighting the grin off her face. "Didn't take you for a fainter."

"I blame your grip on my hand. Snapped every bone I have." I flex my hand and look at my wife, and we both start chuckling weakly. Neither of us has the energy to really laugh.

"I'm sorry for anything I said or did during labor," Elle says, nudging my shoulder.

An exasperated sigh sounds out behind us. The nurse is standing in the doorway. "Didn't I tell you to stay in your bed, Your Majesty?" She shakes her head. "Men—they're all the same." The nurse walks over to the other side of the bed and fiddling with the instruments that are monitoring Elle.

I point to the baby's arm, where baby Charlie's skin is purple and bruised. "What's that?"

"Your wife just pushed this little boy out of her vagina. The baby gets banged up coming out," the nurse explains, not deigning to look at me. "I've seen cone heads, black eyes, full-body bruises. The little Prince had it easy."

She takes Elle's blood pressure, and then puts our son in the bassinet by the bed. I can see it in Elle's face that she doesn't want to let him go, but the exhaustion is lining her face.

I intertwine my fingers in hers and lay my head back on my chair. She curls up on her bed and is asleep in an instant.

The nurse wheels the bassinet over to my side of the bed. She places little Charlie beside me and nods at me. "He's beautiful," she says softly so as to not wake Elle up. "Congratulations, Your Majesty."

Her eyes soften, and she loses all the harshness she had a minute ago. Babies do that to people.

My eyes fill with happy tears and I nod, reaching my other hand over to brush my son's head. "Thank you," I smile.

The nurse leaves the room without another word and I sit there, one hand intertwined with Elle's, and the other holding our son—Farcliff's new heir—and my heart feels so full of happiness it shouldn't be allowed. After everything that's happened to me, I've ended up here with a wife, a baby, and a kingdom to care for.

And I've never felt so happy. Looking at the two people I love most in the world—Elle and my son—I know I wouldn't want it any other way.

~

LILIAN
MONROE

HEARTLESS
PRINCE

ROYALLY UNEXPECTED: **BOOK TWO**

HEARTLESS PRINCE

ROYALLY UNEXPECTED: BOOK 2

Seize the moments of happiness, love and be loved! That is the only reality in the world, all else is folly.

—Leo Tolstoy, War and Peace

1

DAHLIA

I'M CURSED.

Always have been, always will be—but I've learned to live with it.

The barista doesn't know that, though. She just thinks the milk steamer on her espresso machine stopped working as soon as I walked up to the counter.

"Sorry." Her eyebrows arch. "It's never done this before." She glances at the door marked 'Staff Only' behind her, chewing her lip. I wonder if her manager is a hardass.

I shake my head. "It's fine. Forget about the lattes. I'll just have two black coffees."

"I'll refund you."

I smile. "Don't worry about it." I'm not going to punish her just because I'm perpetually unlucky.

Her shoulders relax a bit. She gives me a shy smile. "Okay —thanks."

I take the two coffees to the table where my aunt, Theresa, is waiting. She nods her chin toward the machine, which magically started working again for the next customer.

"What happened?"

"It's the curse."

Auntie T rolls her eyes. "Of course it is. You know there's no curse, right?"

"Try living a day in my shoes and then tell me there's no curse. This morning, I slipped on a banana peel in my kitchen. A banana peel! I don't even eat bananas! Unless this is live-action Mario Kart, that shouldn't happen to a regular person."

"Maybe you're just clumsy," she grins, "and isn't your roommate an athlete? Athletes eat bananas, don't they?"

I huff, sinking down into the chair across from her. The curse is real, and it sabotages me every day. Don't even ask me about my love life—that's in the Oxford English Dictionary under 'disaster'.

My roommate, Elle, would tell you otherwise—but she thinks just because I have a healthy sex life, it means I'm good at dating. I'm not. I've never had a relationship last more than a couple of weeks.

"How was the Prince's Ball, honey?" My aunt asks, bringing her coffee cup to her lips. With an oversized, leopard-print, faux-fur jacket and long crimson nails, she doesn't exactly look like she belongs in the campus café.

I can't meet her eye. I suck at lying—so, I just tell the truth. "I didn't go."

"What? But we received the thank you note from Farcliff Castle. They only send those out if you attend."

I scrunch my napkin between my fingers and take a deep breath. "My roommate went instead of me."

"Why would she do that?" Theresa's painted nails fly to her chest and her bright, red lips drop open. She frowns, as if Elle stole my invitation from me.

Elle didn't steal anything from me. I was the one who convinced her to take my place—and not very easily. She had

274

no desire to go, but I'm glad she did. That's how she met Prince Charlie.

"I didn't want to go, Auntie T. You know how I feel about castles and crowds."

Theresa's eyebrow arches and she looks me up and down. "First of all, you know I don't like it when you call me Auntie. It ages me."

My lips tug into a small smile.

Theresa continues: "Second of all, why would you pass up the chance to go to the Prince's Ball? It only happens once every generation! Are you insane?"

"I didn't feel comfortable going up to the castle."

Theresa tuts, shaking her head. "I blame your mother for this. She scared you away from your own heritage. Why should a Raventhal daughter be afraid of meeting the royal family? It's all this talk about a stupid curse. No one should put those thoughts into a young child's head."

"She's right, though. It's not safe for me there."

Theresa pinches her lips and drums her fingernails on the table. She tilts her head, watching me. "If you're so scared of the castle, why—of all the places where you could study organic chemistry—did you choose Farcliff University?"

"Microbiology."

"What?"

"I study microbiology, not organic chemistry."

"I thought you said..."

"That was just one of my classes last semester."

She waves a dismissive hand. "Whatever. You're avoiding the question. Why come *here*? With your grades, you could have studied anywhere—yet you come to the one place that terrifies you." My aunt purses her lips. "It doesn't make sense for you to come here if you're just going to avoid the royal family. You live in a dumpy house on the edge of Grimdale,

275

and you pretend your last name is Smith. You're a *Raventhal*, Dahlia. You belong up at the castle with the rest of them—so why avoid it?"

I take a sip of coffee and avoid her eyes again. She's right. I live near the edge of the poorer end of the Kingdom called Grimdale—hardly the typical neighborhood for a Raventhal to live. However, it's a perfectly acceptable place for a girl called Smith to live while she studies at Farcliff University.

Growing up, I was hidden away in the forests of the Rocky Mountains. I lived with my three aunts, who served as guardians while my parents lived in exile. I wasn't even told that I was originally from Farcliff until my sixteenth birthday. My parents would come and visit me twice a year, and my mother was the one who'd explained that I'd been cursed as a small baby.

That's why they took me away from Farcliff—to keep me safe from the curse. That's what my mother said, at least. My aunts would shake their heads and tell her to stop putting silly superstitions into my head.

I know how crazy it sounds, but that's the kind of thing that stays with you. Now, I'm supposed to be taking part in court life as if none of that ever happened? As if I haven't been told that going to the castle will kill me?

I sigh. "I don't know. I feel like an imposter. This is where I was born, but I was shipped away from Farcliff when I was a toddler. I never got to see the Raventhal home. Growing up with you, Aunt Helen, and Aunt Margie was..."

I trail off, lost in my own thoughts.

"It was what?" Theresa's voice has an edge to it.

I take a deep breath. "It was wonderful. I loved growing up in the wild. I loved being surrounded by nature and birds —even if being allergic to pollen, and bees, and insect bites isn't exactly convenient in the middle of the wilderness. Even so, it was peaceful. But... I don't know who I am, Theresa. All of a sudden, when I turned sixteen, you told me I was a Raventhal and that I belonged in the Farcliff Court. I just want..." I sigh, shrugging. "I don't know what I want."

I sip my coffee as Theresa studies me. When she doesn't say anything, I know she wants me to keep talking.

"Whenever I see Mom, she always tells me they're dangerous at court. And then you're telling me the opposite —pushing me towards it, telling me it's fine. Which is it? Is it safe, or not safe? Am I cursed, or not cursed?"

Theresa puts her hand over mine. Her face softens as she gently squeezes my fingers. "Your mother has her own ideas. I'm just trying to encourage you to be the Lady you were born to be. I want you to reach your full potential, Dahlia."

I take a deep breath. "I know Mom has always been paranoid about the Farcliff royal family. I don't want to live in fear like she does."

"So, why are you running away from it? Why not go up to the castle when you're invited?"

"It scares me. What happened with Mom..."

"What happened with your mother was unfortunate, but I don't know if it was really as bad as she thought. It was more of a scandal in the press than anything truly dangerous."

"You mean her exile?" I stare at my aunt and take a deep breath. "What exactly happened with her? All I know is that the Queen died, and Mom started claiming she'd been murdered—and then she was sent away. Whenever I ask her about it, she clams up."

Now, it's Theresa's turn to avoid my gaze. She stares out of the window at the stream of students walking toward their classes. "That's more or less what happened," she says.

"More or less? What does that mean?"

My aunt sighs. "It's not for me to tell, munchkin."

"Why not?"

"It was a long time ago, Dahlia. It doesn't matter anymore."

Frustration builds inside me until I feel like I'm going to explode. This happens every time I try to find out about the past. Whether I ask my aunts or my parents, I always get the same answer. It's in the past. I'm not old enough. It's not for them to tell.

Well, whose story *is* it to tell? How am I supposed to know who to trust in Farcliff if I don't know what happened, or why my mother was exiled? She used to be the Queen's best friend —now, I can't even ask anyone why that changed.

"The King's sister was spearheading the campaign to have your mother exiled," Theresa explains. She pinches her lips together and her lipstick creases. Her eyes tighten as she stares at me, and I hold my breath. No one has ever said anything about this to me before.

"The King's sister?"

"Lady Malerie." Theresa sighs. "She never liked your mother. I think Mal was insulted that the Queen asked your mother to be a bridesmaid and not her. Said she was the King's sister, and Tabitha Raventhal was a nobody. Very easily offended, that woman." Theresa tuts her lips and shakes her head. "Lots of drama surrounding her."

"I never heard about this."

"No," Theresa answers without explanation.

"So... Exiling Mom was payback? For not being asked to be a bridesmaid?"

"The bridesmaid thing started it all... And then there was Prince Charlie's christening. Phew! Don't get me started on *that*." Theresa shakes her head. "When Tabitha was named godmother instead of Lady Malerie? Well—all hell broke loose."

My heart thumps. No one has ever been this open with me before. I lean forward. "What happened at Charlie's christening?"

My question seems to snap Theresa out of her own thoughts. She looks at me, wide-eyed, and inhales sharply. She claps her hands together and shakes her head. "What are we doing, talking about things that don't matter? I'm here to take you out to lunch! We should be pampering ourselves, not talking about silly drama from the past."

"What if I want to talk about silly drama?"

"Well, that may be, but we have some self-care to attend to. Come on, I didn't come all the way from Colorado to visit my darling niece just to spend the whole time sitting in a cramped coffee shop. I've made us an appointment with Farcliff's best hairdresser. Your colors need some refreshing, and I need a blowout."

I run my hands through my multicolored strands and take a deep breath. I can tell by the look on Theresa's face that I won't be getting any more information out of her today.

Besides, my hair is dyed a rainbow of pastel colors, and Theresa is right—it does need a refresh. Sighing, I give in. She's told me something, at least. I can look into Lady Malerie, the King's sister. Maybe that will give me some clues as to where I come from, why my family was thrown out of Farcliff, and where this whole idea of a curse came from.

Aunt Theresa throws her arm around my shoulder and leads me out of the café just as my two other aunts, Helen and Margie, come screeching down the street in my orange Jeep. Helen has a bright blue headscarf on, paired with over-sized glasses, and Margie's long mane of silver hair whips wildly around her head. They whoop and holler toward us as everyone on the street turns to stare.

Theresa tugs me toward the Jeep and I let a smile slide

279

over my lips. My aunts taught me to live a loud, happy, colorful life. They were the best guardians I could have asked for—but I can't keep shying away from the questions that plague me. I can't keep living in fear of a curse that might not even exist.

I need to know where I come from, and what happened with my family all those years ago.

~

ALSO BY LILIAN MONROE

For all books, visit:

www.lilianmonroe.com

Brother's Best Friend Romance

Shouldn't Want You

Can't Have You

Don't Need You

Won't Miss You

Military Romance

His Vow

His Oath

His Word

The Complete Protector Series

Enemies to Lovers Romance

Hate at First Sight

Loathe at First Sight

Despise at First Sight

The Complete Love/Hate Series

Secret Baby/Accidental Pregnancy Romance:

Knocked Up by the CEO

Knocked Up by the Single Dad

Knocked Up...Again!

Knocked Up by the Billionaire's Son

The Complete Unexpected Series

Yours for Christmas

Bad Prince

Heartless Prince

Cruel Prince

Broken Prince

Wicked Prince

Wrong Prince

Fake Engagement/ Fake Marriage Romance:

Engaged to Mr. Right

Engaged to Mr. Wrong

Engaged to Mr. Perfect

Mr Right: The Complete Fake Engagement Series

Mountain Man Romance:

Lie to Me

Swear to Me

Run to Me

The Complete Clarke Brothers Series

Extra-Steamy Rock Star Romance:

Garrett

Maddox

Carter

The Complete Rock Hard Series

Sexy Doctors:

Doctor O

Doctor D

Doctor L

The Complete Doctor's Orders Series

Time Travel Romance:

The Cause

A little something different:

Second Chance: A Rockstar Romance in North Korea